The Burning

The Burning

J.P. Seewald

AnnorlundaBooks

Dedicated to the people of Centralia, Pennsylvania, whose real-life plight inspired this work of fiction.

CHAPTER ONE

The hard coal country of Eastern Pennsylvania, 1975

"So, when Mr. Kessler broke up the fight in the cafeteria today, he asked Jeff Haskins why he kicked Richie Nash in the stomach. Jeff said it wasn't his fault. Richie turned around suddenly." Jimmy's narrative made George Ferris laugh. George was proud of the way his thirteen-year-old son could tell vivid stories. No question about it, Jimmy was a lively kid, using hand gestures and changing voice inflections when he spoke. George didn't fail to notice that his son was dressed like him in plaid flannel shirt and jeans. He took it as a sign of respect.

"That sounds just like what a Haskins would say." George turned to his brother, Larry. "Remember when Tim Haskins nailed you from behind?"

Larry frowned. "How could I forget?"

Jimmy's expression was animated. "What happened? Was it a big fight?"

"Your dad told Tim he'd have to battle him first. That ended it."

"Bet you were pretty tough in those days," Jimmy said, looking up at George.

"I've still got a few moves left in me." He began to wrestle jokingly with his son. "Jimmy thinks I'm over the hill," George told Larry as he let his son up from the living room floor.

"Were you in a lot of fights when you were a kid, Dad?" Jimmy raised his brows.

"I never started any, but I ended a few."

"The terminator?"

"Your dad never was beaten," Larry said.

"Except by your Uncle Larry, but he didn't do it with his fists." George glanced over at Larry and thought how his brother looked every inch the successful attorney that he was. Larry wore gold-framed glasses, expensive designer suit, shirt and tie. His haircut was professionally styled. He projected a well-groomed image that George realized looked out of place in his homey, blue-collar living room.

"So the Haskins kid got in trouble for fighting?" George shook his head.

Larry's wife, Suzanne, entered the living room, glanced at George, frowned, and began pacing while puffing on a cigarette.

"The more things change, the more they stay the same." Seemed as though he never saw Suzanne without a cancer stick in her hand.

Suzanne turned to him. "What an original thought. Maybe you missed your calling, George. You could have been a maharishi."

"Did you say something, Suzanne?"

She ignored his question and took a long drag on her cigarette. Typical Suzanne tactic.

"Honey, why don't you join us?" Larry patted the couch seat next to him.

"I'd rather not." Suzanne lifted her chin and pursed her lips as if she'd been sucking on a lemon.

Larry turned to George. "Let's discuss something Suzanne is interested in."

"Sure." George called out to his sister-in-law. "Didn't they open some new stores at the shopping mall recently?" He couldn't seem to keep the sarcasm out of his voice.

"I wouldn't know."

"I thought shopping was your calling."

Suzanne absently flicked ashes at a drinking glass. "I have no idea what you are talking about." She then approached George and blew smoke in his face.

"So what *are* you doing with yourself these days?" George asked.

"I manage to keep busy."

"Well, that's good. It could get boring with so little to do and so much time on your hands."

Why did Suzanne have to make it so obvious that she hated being in his house? It was hard to believe that his brother had married such a snob. He and Suzanne had disliked each other from the first time they'd met, and George was certain that was never going to change. He remembered how she'd looked down her long nose at his parents, as if she was honoring them with her presence. Yet still they'd welcomed her with warmth and had tried to make her feel at home. People like Suzanne were never satisfied. They always wanted and expected more material things, never appreciated humble kindness. George would never accept Suzanne's attitude. He supposed it was a failing of his nature not to be as accepting as his parents had been. He probably should have been more like them and his wife, a woman who always saw the best in other people.

Larry loosened his tie as if it were a noose and cleared his throat. "Suzanne's been very involved in physical fitness lately."

"No kidding. That's very big, isn't it?"

"Suz joined a health club where she can swim year round, get massages, work out on machines, take aerobics and dance classes. She's even got a terrific trainer who provides her with individual attention."

"That so? Do you go with her, Lar?"

"No, it's strictly for women. Suz goes during the day while I'm working."

George turned to Suzanne, who was doing her best to ignore the conversation. "Say, maybe you could take Liz with you sometime. She'd love a place like that."

"Oh, I hardly think so. Besides, it's rather far from here."

George refused to be daunted. "Still, Liz could go with you once in a while."

Suzanne scrunched her nose in annoyance. "It's really not her sort of place. She wouldn't fit in."

Larry's face reddened in embarrassment. "What Suzanne means is that Liz likes to be here when the kids get home from school. She couldn't do that if she went off with Suzanne."

Suzanne turned on her husband. "Dearest, don't tell me what I mean."

Liz entered the room carrying a coffee tray. He found himself comparing his wife to his sister-in-law. Liz was more attractive, even dressed in plain, casual clothes unlike Suzanne. Her hair was her own natural dark brown color with auburn highlights that caught the lamplight. In sharp contrast, Suzanne's short hair was bleached blond and stiffly sprayed. She was wearing heavy make-up and expensive gold jewelry. George couldn't help observing that Suzanne in her fancy dress seemed clearly out of place in their house, even more so than his brother.

Amy followed behind her mother carrying a plate of cookies. Liz and Amy set their offerings down on the scarred coffee table. His heart filled with love for both of them.

"Amy, you look like you've grown taller since the last time I saw you," Larry said. "Let's see. You're almost eleven, aren't you?"

"I'll be eleven in two months, but Jimmy says I'm a shrimp." She threw her brother an accusing look.

"Hey, I only said that when you were being annoying."

"That's enough, you two," Liz admonished. "I hope we're all ready for some dessert."

"I'm already full," Larry said, patting his stomach. "That was a terrific meal. No one cooks pot roast the way you do, Liz."

George smiled, pleased by his brother's comment. "She said it was your favorite. That's why she made it."

Liz cast her eyes downward, as if embarrassed by the compliment.

Larry turned a warm smile on Liz. "Thank you."

"I got a joke for you, Uncle Larry," Jimmy said. The freckles on his nose appeared to dance.

Liz narrowed her eyes. "Jimmy!"

"Mom, it's a clean one. Honor bright." Jimmy raised his right hand.

Liz placed her hands on her hips. "Isn't it time for you to finish your homework?"

Jimmy lifted his chin. "Come on, I got very little left."

George inclined his head. "Seems to me that's what you say every night, kiddo."

Larry intervened. "Let him stay a while. I rarely get to spend time with my niece and nephew these days."

"Got too many clients," George said.

Larry smiled. "You can never have too many."

Suzanne placed her hand on Larry's shoulder. "You know what Wally Simpson said? 'You can never be too rich or too thin.' Larry's doing fabulously, thanks to all the contacts he made through Daddy."

Larry shrugged off his wife's hands. He seemed irritated by Suzanne's snotty comment. Who wouldn't?

"Right, haven't had to chase an ambulance in years." Larry turned his attention to Amy. "So how have you been?"

Amy sat down beside her uncle on the couch. "Oh fine, Uncle Larry."

"Your dad tells me that you were elected president of your class and that you have straight A's."

George swelled with pride. "My little girl's

really something special." He bent over and kissed her forehead.

Amy's cheeks flushed. "Dad, you shouldn't brag about me. It's no big deal making the honor roll. Lots of kids do it."

Amy started to cough and had difficulty stopping. Liz placed her arms around their daughter and looked over at Suzanne meaningfully.

Suzanne glanced down at her cigarette. "Is she allergic to smoke?"

Liz's mouth tightened. "Amy has asthma. I thought you knew that."

Suzanne offered an uncomfortable shrug.

Liz exited the living room with her arm still around Amy while Suzanne quickly stubbed out her cigarette.

Guiltily, George realized he should have told Suzanne to put out her cigarette the moment he saw her smoking in his house. "It's a little close in here. Suppose I open a window." He got up and went to open the window.

Suzanne threw him a hard look. "Good idea, nothing like getting frostbite."

Larry frowned at her. "Suz, the room was getting stuffy."

Suzanne glanced around. "Old houses like this are always musty and moldy." She ran her fingers along the edge of the coffee table as if to brush away some imagined dust.

"Old houses have more character." George appreciated his brother's comment. Larry must still feel the same close family connection with their family home.

Suzanne patted her unmoving bleached blond hair. "I don't know about that."

"I bet you don't," George said.

Suzanne tossed him a killing look.

"George, remember when Mom and Dad first took us to see this place?"

"Yeah, I loved it right away. I still remember the day they put the down payment together, every cent they could scrimp."

Larry let out a sigh. "This house meant so much to them."

"To all of us. I'm grateful the kids could grow up here, just the way we did."

"That's why Mom left you the house. She knew."

George looked at his brother. "You sure didn't need it! Your place is a mansion, a freakin' palace. Makes the White House look shabby."

Larry held up his hands as if warding off evil spirits. "Hey, don't exaggerate. Anyway, it's Suzanne's house."

Suzanne placed her hand on his shoulder again. "Our house, darling."

Larry looked up at her, his gray eyes owlishly round through his gold-rimmed glasses. "Your father paid for it."

Liz and Amy rejoined them in the living room.

"So what were you talking about while we were out in the kitchen?"

Larry smiled at Liz. "Just discussing what Suz does all day while I'm hard at work."

Suzanne folded her arms over her chest. "According to George, shopping. He believes I've made a career of it. I'm sure he got that foolish idea from Larry." She bent over and kissed her husband on the cheek. "Larry likes to tease me about my self-indulgence, my little extravagances, just because I believe that a woman should take care of herself and have an up-to-date wardrobe."

"Let's see: Last week, you had a facial, your hair and nails done, went for a pedicure, a massage and—"

Suzanne said, "Really, Larry, I don't get the works every week. I need to pamper myself a little. Living out here in the boonies, there's nothing of interest to do."

Larry shrugged. "This is where I work."

"You're hardly a hick country lawyer, dear. You spend half your time in Harrisburg or Philadelphia, while I'm entombed out here, practically dead in Dinkyville. And all my friends live so far away."

"We have the phone bills to prove it."

"Life out here is so dull. I miss the excitement and cultural stimulation of living in the city."

"What do you think, Liz?" Larry turned to her.

"I'm pretty busy most of the time, but I can understand how Suzanne must feel. Although I'm not a city girl, even I have my moments. There are times when I wouldn't mind going back to work, at least part-time."

George lifted his head and stared at her. "That's news to me." Was Liz dissatisfied with her life? He hoped not.

"Well, the kids are in school all day. The

housework doesn't take all my time." Liz sounded defensive.

Suzanne arched her brows. "I suppose someone can always use a file clerk."

Liz threw her sister-in-law a hard look. "I was a legal secretary."

"Of course. You might do what some of my friends consider fulfilling." Suzanne stared at her blood-red fingernails.

"What might that be?"

Suzanne looked up. "They donate time to worthy causes, but you probably want to earn extra money."

George clenched his teeth. "My wife doesn't need to work."

Suzanne looked uneasy. Maybe she understood she'd gone too far, but George doubted it. Someone like Suzanne had a sense of entitlement.

"Perhaps I'll just freshen up." Suzanne grabbed her purse and hurried toward the bathroom off the hallway.

Amy turned to Larry. "Can I show you the parakeet that Mom and Dad got me for me?"

"Sure, I'd love to see it."

"It's the only parakeet I ever heard that sings off-key," Jimmy said.

Amy smacked his arm. "That's not true. Take it back!"

"Come on, Amy, it was just a joke."

Larry looked from Amy to Jimmy. "Okay, my turn to tell a joke. This is one only I can tell because it's about lawyers. Why didn't the shark eat the lawyer when he fell off the boat?"

Amy shook her head. "I don't know."

"Professional courtesy."

Jimmy groaned. "That's a real old one, Uncle Larry."

Larry smiled. "Okay, smart guy, your turn."

George watched the three of them go off to the kitchen then turned to Liz and spoke softly, "What do you want to bet Suzanne is smoking in the john?"

"George!"

"That woman's a human ashtray. She may have come a long way, baby, but as far as I'm concerned, it's not far enough."

Liz folded her hands together. "You could be misjudging her, you know."

George shook his head. "Get real. You think they'll leave soon?"

Liz let out an exasperated sigh. "Larry's your brother, and you did the inviting."

George rolled his eyes. "Yeah, I know, and I do enjoy being with Larry, but Suzanne gets on my nerves. Everything's been handed to her. She's spoiled rotten, a rich bitch. I don't like her one bit."

Liz touched his hand. "I think you've made that pretty clear. The two of you rub each other the wrong way. I'm sure she's got problems, just like everyone."

George licked his lips, which felt dry. "Like what?"

"Well, for instance, I think she's basically very insecure. That's probably why she acts the way she does."

"Insecure? For Christ's sake, what would she have to be insecure about? My brother puts that woman on a pedestal. He can't do enough for her, not that she appreciates it."

Liz rubbed her arms, her dark brown eyes unfocused, as if she were lost in thought. "Still, she's not happy. I can see that. Let's give her the benefit of a doubt. Okay?"

Larry strode back into the room, his pace slow, his hands in his jacket pockets, his expression thoughtful.

Liz turned to him. "Will you have a cup of coffee?"

"No, thanks. I've got an early schedule tomorrow morning. I think we're going to have to leave."

George let out a sigh of relief as Suzanne returned to the living room.

"What about you, Suzanne, would you like some coffee?"

"It keeps me awake at night if I have caffeine in the evening. I don't need my nerves jangling any more than they already do. I'm sleep-challenged as it is."

Larry glanced at his gold Rolex. "We better get going."

George rose to his feet. "Seems like we hardly had a chance to talk." He regretted the distance that had developed between him and his brother, and yet he'd be glad to see Larry and his wife leave. The evening had been awkward all around.

"I'll be by the station tomorrow. We'll talk then."

George nodded. "I'll get your coats."

Larry turned to Liz. "Once again, thank you for going to so much trouble for us."

Liz seemed to light up. "No big deal. It was our pleasure."

They smiled warmly at each other, and then Liz lowered her eyes. Suzanne also noticed the look that had passed between them and glanced away as if upset.

Larry took Liz's hand and held it for a moment. "Say goodnight to the kids for us. Maybe we can have you folks over soon."

Suzanne's face colored. She looked flustered. "Yes, the new housekeeper is working out well. She does some interesting ethnic dishes, or is the politically correct word multi-cultural?"

George fetched the coats from the front hall closet then handed them to Larry, who helped Suzanne with hers before he put on his own.

Larry shook his hand. "Good night."

He gave Liz a quick peck on the cheek, then took Suzanne's arm and departed.

Liz brushed her hand against her face, touching her cheek where Larry had kissed it. "George, let's not have them over again for a while."

"Sure." He studied her thoughtfully then placed his arm around her. "Whatever you want, I agree." An ominous chill slithered down his back. Maybe he wasn't the sharpest guy when it came to picking up on emotions, but something had passed between his brother and his wife, even if just for a moment. And he didn't like it one bit.

CHAPTER TWO

George wiped sweat from his brow then glanced around him. This town was his home. True, it wasn't much to look at, set in a barren valley that provided coal for industry. The coal came at a price in human life. Neither George nor his brother made their livelihood from coal mining. Their father had urged them both against it. The old man had been wise to that extent. George was grateful for his father's advice, and yet he still couldn't help feeling dissatisfied.

Larry was standing beside his car while George pumped gas into it. George rolled up the sleeves of his denim work shirt, aware that it was none too clean. Larry, as usual, was dressed in an expensive navy business suit, conservatively tailored, that screamed class. It brought home once again the different paths he and his brother's lives had taken.

George ran his hand along the sleek, polished hood of Larry's automobile, admiring his brother's taste in cars. "So how's the BMW running?"

"Much better since you worked on it last time."

George shrugged. "By rights you should have taken it to the dealership."

"Nobody there will care for my car the way you do."

"Good to hear. Thanks for the vote of confidence." It pleased him to know that Larry valued his mechanical ability.

"You have a way with automobiles."

"My theory is that a car should handle like a responsive woman."

"Maybe I ought to bring Suzanne in for a tune-up."

George laughed. "'Fraid I only know how to work with cars. Dealing with people is more in your line."

Larry's expression darkened. "Sometimes I wonder about that."

Talking about their wives possibly wasn't such a good idea. "Saw your name in the newspaper again. I felt proud of you."

Larry's face flushed with what seemed like

embarrassment "I did manage to get a good settlement for a client, but he had a strong case. Most lawyers would have done as well."

"You're so damn modest. Why, if the old man were still alive, he'd be bragging all over town about you."

"I doubt it. Our father wasn't one to brag. Personally, I think that just makes enemies."

George slapped his brother on the back. "You inspire me, you know that? I'm going to see to it that Jimmy gets a real good education just like you."

Larry's expression turned thoughtful. "It's best to let him do whatever makes him happy."

"Kids don't know what's best for them. They need someone to steer them in the right direction. I don't plan on letting Jimmy make the same mistakes I did."

Larry narrowed his eyes. "What mistakes? You can fix anything. You're the best mechanic around. A man should feel proud when he does a job well. Not everyone can or will."

George smiled ruefully at the compliment then he topped off the gas tank and replaced the cap. "I had to be good, just to stay in the running."

Larry threw up his hands. "I didn't know there was a contest."

"Between you and me? Always. Maybe you didn't know it because you won without even trying."

Larry pulled at his shirt collar. He seemed unwilling to comment further. George probably shouldn't have said what he had to make Larry feel uncomfortable, but George took pride in being honest. He wasn't going to change at the age of forty-four just to spare his brother's feelings.

Larry looked at the gas meter then pulled out his wallet from which he removed a credit card. He then handed it to George.

"I'll get your bill filled out."

George started to walk inside the station, but momentarily lost his balance. For some strange reason, he felt dizzy. He stumbled and nearly fell. Larry came forward to lend support, placing his arms around George.

"What's wrong?" Larry's voice rose in alarm.

George placed his hand to his head and walked on unsteadily.

"Just felt a little dizzy for a second, is all. I'm all right now."

Larry furrowed his brow. "Has this happened before?"

George felt embarrassed. He disliked showing any signs of weakness, especially in front of his brother. "Couple of times lately. It's nothing."

But Larry continued to hold on to his arm. "Meaning that lately you've been feeling sick?"

"Counselor is leading the witness."

"This isn't anything to joke about. Let's go into your office and give you a chance to sit down for a few minutes." George wasn't up to arguing with Larry. They went to his office.

"Look, I'm okay. I'll make out your credit slip." He did his best to ignore the nausea vortexing through his gut. He'd felt dizzy several times lately but never this bad. Still, he could shake it off like he'd done before.

Larry physically stopped him from working, forcing George to sit down in the chair behind his desk.

"What are you doing? I told you. I'm okay."

"I'm making sure you take it easy for a few seconds. Don't you think you ought to visit Doc Holmes? How long's it been since you had a check-up?"

George was becoming irritated. He didn't want Larry fussing over him, maybe thinking him weak. "I said I'm okay. Don't make a big deal over nothing."

"You won't know whether or not something's wrong until you get checked over. Why don't I call and make the appointment for you right now?" Larry reached over for the telephone on the desk, but George stopped him from dialing, grabbing him.

"Hey, don't break my arm."

George released him. "Look, I know you have my best interests at heart, but I'm the big brother, remember? So stop being so bossy. I'm fine. When I'm ready, I'll call myself. I don't need you to insist I get a check-up. Understood?"

"Okay, but will you do it?"

"I said I would." George felt like punching his brother. Larry meant well but could be overbearing and annoying at times. "Just because I didn't go to college like you, it doesn't mean I'm stupid. When I think I need to see a doctor, I will."

"All right, just don't take too long getting around to it. Say, are you aware of how awful it smells in here? No wonder you're feeling rotten. The odor in this place could drop a moose."

"What do you expect in a gas station, for Christ's sake, perfume and roses?

"Place is an armpit," Larry said frowning.

"Part of the ambiance."

"We need to get some fresh air in here."

Larry started to open the closest window. As he did so, his hand brushed against the wall. He retracted it instantly then cautiously placed his hand back on the wall experimentally at different locations.

"George, are you aware your walls are burning hot?"

George blinked in surprise. "You kidding me?"

"Wish I were."

George got up and touched each wall just as Larry had done. He couldn't believe it. "Christ, they are hot! What could be causing it?"

"I don't know, but we're going to have to find out, and quick!" Larry raised the telephone receiver and punched in some numbers.

George sat down heavily in his chair. What was going on here?

CHAPTER THREE

The following day, George was apprehensive. He had a sense of déjà vu because Larry again stood beside him near the pumps at his gas station. The only difference was that a Mr. Baines of the State Department of Environmental Protection had joined them. George disliked bureaucrats. He found them in general to be self-serving and shifty. Baines had hard eyes and struck George as a typical bureaucrat, a balding fiftyish guy, dressed in a dark business suit with a demeanor both stern and aloof. No, he didn't like this cold fish one bit.

Baines turned to him, clipboard in hand. "I've completed my investigation, Mr. Ferris."

George's throat tightened with anxiety. He swallowed hard, his mouth dry. "What did you find out?"

Baines looked down at his clipboard. It was a bad sign that the man didn't meet his gaze. "I'll be blunt and get right to the point. Your service station has to be shut down."

George's mouth dropped open in disbelief. His heart began beating rapidly. He wasn't sure what he'd expected to hear but it wasn't that. "What are you talking about? That's crazy! There's nothing wrong with this place. Everything in this garage is in first-class condition."

Baines continued to avoid his eyes. "Not quite everything."

Baines turns to Larry. "I'm afraid your brother doesn't understand the situation."

Larry lifted his chin. "Frankly, neither do I."

Baines turned back to George. "If your station isn't closed down immediately, then everyone in this vicinity will be in terrible danger. The temperature in your underground storage tanks has risen to over 170 degrees Fahrenheit. The gasoline has got to be drained from all your tanks otherwise there'll be a massive explosion. Is that clear enough?"

George's hands began to shake. He was unable to control them. His heart beat so hard he could barely catch his breath. His gas station blowing up? Could that really happen? "I don't believe it!"

"Well, I'm afraid it's true."

"But you can't expect me to close my business. This is my livelihood you're talking about! Damn it, I've poured my life's blood into this place."

Larry placed a restraining hand on George's arm then he turned to Baines. "You better explain what's happening here. I thought you environmental protection people were supposed to be on our side."

Baines let out a deep sigh. "We are on your side, and we do whatever we can to help. This is a difficult situation. Have you gentlemen been aware there's a coal fire burning underground? Apparently it's spread very near the spot where we are standing."

George was confused. "Coal fire? What coal fire?"

Larry gave an alert nod. "Are you talking about the fire that got started about eighteen years ago?"

Baines pursed his lips. "I believe it was around then."

George shook his head. "I don't remember hearing about it."

Larry turned to him. "It started just about the time you were in the army. Someone torched the garbage dump. We all figured it was teenage vandals up to their usual pranks. No one ever admitted to setting it. By the time the fire company managed to stamp it out, some coal under the surface had ignited. It spread to one of the coal seams and then into the mines, forcing them to shut down operation. That's when Pop stopped working."

George bit down on his lower lip. "Just as well, considering what the coal dust did to his lungs." He hadn't forgotten his father coughing uncontrollably, spitting up blood.

Larry continued, "Anyway, the fire's been burning in the abandoned mine shafts ever since."

George took a deep breath and let it out slowly, trying to think with a clear head. "I can't believe it could actually spread this far." It was difficult for George to process all this bewildering information. It seemed confusing and unreal.

Baines viewed him without expression. "No one cared enough to see that the fire was put out. What people don't see, they don't worry about. Isn't that right, Mr. Ferris?"

The way Baines was talking to him made George furious. "Don't try to put the blame for this on me."

Larry placed a restraining hand on his shoulder then turned again to confront Baines. "You're oversimplifying the situation. It's a lot more complex than that."

"Really?" Baines didn't bother hiding his skepticism.

Larry narrowed his gaze. He was half a head taller than Baines and looked down on the man. "There was an attempt to put out the fire a few years back, but the town ran out of money. The fire department didn't have proper equipment. It's strictly done on a volunteer basis. The mayor and town council couldn't agree about appropriating enough funds. Even then, it seemed like a considerable sum of money. More than the town could afford. There's not much money here, you know. This has always been a poor, coal-mining town."

Baines appeared unmoved. "Are you certain a true effort was made?"

George hated the man's condescending attitude. "I guess Larry didn't tell you: He serves as lawyer to the mayor and the town council. You're looking at a very well-informed man." George placed his arm around his brother. "When Larry says something, he speaks with authority. You can always rely on him to tell the truth."

Larry tugged at his shirt collar as if it felt too

tight. "Look, what about you people? Can we get some assistance from the state? Will your department at least try to help us?"

"We've already studied the problem. Your brother's not the first to be effected, Mr. Ferris. The fact is, it would take one hundred million dollars to put out the fire."

George let out a low whistle. "That much?"

Baines appeared unmoved, his face devoid of expression or emotion. "That's right. Naturally, the state isn't willing to pay all of it."

Larry shook his head. "Well, there's no way that the town could foot the bill. What about the federal government? Will EPA help us?"

Baines started to walk away, with George following close behind. "We've already discussed the possibility of matching funds. They turned a deaf ear to us."

George breathed heavily. "How can that be? I pay my taxes."

Baines gifted him with a twisted smile. "Our rich uncle in Washington is a trifle parsimonious, I'm afraid."

George shoved his hands into his jeans pockets. It was a chilly April day but he found himself sweating. What was he supposed to do? He needed to save his business, his livelihood. He wished he were smarter and could figure out a solution, but all he felt was a sense of confusion. "Where does that leave me?"

Baines turned and looked at him directly for the first time. "The bottom line? Just as I told you. Closing down your business immediately, Mr. Ferris, before your gasoline combusts and causes an explosion."

George couldn't accept that callous pronouncement. "Politicians gotta have hearts."

Baines smiled coldly. "Only during election years. Then they make empty promises they have no intention of making good on once they get into office." Baines picked up his pace, hurrying toward his shiny black sedan.

"I can't believe that no one is willing to help. It makes no sense to me." George clutched his midsection. He was doing his best not to throw up.

Larry looked just as stunned. "We're talking about a natural disaster. Surely my brother is not alone? Couldn't everyone affected be helped as a group?"

Baines momentarily appeared to relent. "I can't say, but I'll look into it. To be blunt, the general opinion is that the people in this community created the situation themselves by being apathetic at the inception of the problem."

Larry placed a hand on the bureaucrat's forearm, halting his departure. "And are you of a similar opinion?"

Baines looked at Larry then at George. "As a matter of fact, I am. I'm afraid that you can expect very little sympathy or aid from the state or federal government."

George felt as if he'd been punched. He nearly doubled over. "State or federal, DEP, EPA, what's the difference? You're all making an A-S-S out of me!"

Larry placed his arm around George's shoulder in a gesture of support. "Mr. Baines, your assessment seems callous."

Baines gave an indifferent shrug. George supposed he'd given similar news before, and like a doctor dealing with terminal patients, he'd developed a hard shell. "I'm only doing my job. Don't start portioning out blame."

"Funny, I had the distinct feeling that was exactly what you were doing." Though Larry was good with words, it wasn't helping.

"Where does that leave me?" George said. He

knew he was repeating himself but couldn't seem to help it.

Baines scowled at him. "For the time being, you must see to closing down your business. I'll be in contact. I'll also be back to make certain everything has been taken care of correctly. Good day, gentlemen."

George shook his head as he watched Baines drive away. He wished he could deny what was happening. It was like a nightmare from which he couldn't wake. "Damn it, what am I going to do? I'm screwed!"

Larry again placed a comforting arm around him. "We'll think of something. This isn't the end. We'll wait until after the inspection and talk with Baines some more."

George was torn between hope and despair. He wanted to believe Larry's words but deep down expected the suits to screw him. Didn't that always happen to ordinary working guys like him? "You really think that will do any good?"

"I don't know, but at least we can try. I plan to discuss this with the mayor and the council. Maybe we can work something out. We can talk to the state commission and the federal government about getting some help too. I can arrange for publicity. Winning public support can make a difference."

Larry would do everything he could to help. That mattered to George. "Thanks, I appreciate your support. You're a great brother."

"I don't know about that, but I'll do my best. Just try to keep calm. Things will work out, one way or another."

But which way would that be? George let out an involuntary shudder. He looked back at his gas station. It had meant so much to him when he was finally able to open his own shop and work on cars for himself. No more bosses. His investment and commitment had been total. Now what was going to happen? It was just starting to hit him, the deep sense of loss, losing what he'd been working for all these years. Was it truly gone? He wasn't a man given to displays of strong emotion, but his despair and grief made him feel like breaking down in tears. No, he wouldn't give in to those feelings, wouldn't let them overwhelm him, no matter what.

CHAPTER FOUR

George drove home on autopilot, detached, barely aware of his surroundings. The talk with Baines kept turning over in his head. He'd worked so hard for so many years to provide a good life for his family. Was that going to end now? The whole thing seemed crazy. Could some underground fire wreck his life and that of his family? He shook his head, refusing to accept this as inevitable.

The living room of George Ferris's house usually offered a refuge, but he didn't want to walk inside yet. Instead he stood in the front hallway praying for composure while silently lurking. He could see Amy was sitting on the sofa attentively reading a book, feet tucked under her.

Every so often, she coughed. Liz came into the room. She was dressed in brown slacks and a casual cream-colored blouse. He admired how beautiful his wife was. With her natural good looks, she wore very little make-up and didn't need it. George was reminded of how much he loved her. Liz was the real deal. What would this news do to her? She deserved so much better in life. For a few minutes, he watched Liz straightening up the room, but then she stopped to listen to Amy's recurring cough.

"Amy, how long has Doc Holmes had you on that medicine?"

Amy shrugged. "I don't know exactly, Mom. About six months I guess. Why?"

"Because it doesn't seem to be helping. Maybe we should ask for a change of prescription."

"Mom, you worry too much. You know my allergies are always worse in the spring."

Liz bit down on her lower lip. "It hasn't even gotten warm yet. I'm going to ask Doc Holmes to switch the medication. These past few days, it seems you can hardly catch your breath."

"I'll be all right. Wish you wouldn't worry so much."

"Is it such a sin for me to be concerned about you? Do you have any idea how much you mean to me?" Liz put her arms around their daughter and hugged her.

Amy pulled away. "Caring too much is as bad as caring too little."

"I sometimes forget. You've reached the age where you know more than I do."

"All I meant was you overprotect me. It's kind of like being smothered by a soft pillow."

Jimmy entered the room, having come in through the back, the mud room. George knew how much Jimmy loved the yard and preferred the outdoors. He was dressed in a football jersey and jeans, and George thought his son looked every bit like an athlete. Jimmy dropped his books carelessly on the coffee table and tossed his jacket on the floor.

Liz's face flushed with indignation. "Just a minute, young man, I am not your maid! Pick up that jacket and put your books away."

Jimmy hung his head. "Sorry, Mom." He picked up his jacket and books, putting them on a chair. "Is that better?"

She frowned at him. "Not much. Put everything where it belongs."

George smiled to himself. Jimmy was a typical boy but he'd have to learn self-discipline.

"How's school?"

"I batted a homer and drove in the winning run in our scrimmage today. Know what else? The coach thinks I'm a natural for football too. He says I got all the right moves for a running back. I can hardly wait 'til I start high school. I can go out for football in the fall and baseball in the spring."

"I'm more interested in how you did on that science test."

Jimmy lowered his eyes. "Oh that!" He paused. "Well, I guess I sort of flunked it."

"Jimmy, your father's going to be so upset!"

That was true. After the day he'd had, George hated hearing more bad news.

"Why does he have to know about it?"

Liz shook her head in annoyance. "I don't think your father's made any secret about wanting you to get a good education. I wish you could manage to spend more time studying. You seem to want to do everything else but. Next year, young man, you're entering the big time. Those grades count, and if they're not good, you can't go to college."

Jimmy ran his fingers through his shock of sandy hair. "Except for gym and shop, I'm not good in school. I can't stand the worthless junk we're supposed to learn."

Liz stamped her foot. "It's not worthless."

Jimmy faced her. They were the same height.

Jimmy was becoming tall. "All right, then it's just dull."

"What about your dad? Are you going to disappoint him?"

Jimmy stood his ground. "Dad hasn't been in school for a long time. He forgot what it's like. I want to learn to fix cars the way he does. Amy's the one who ought to go to college."

"We want both of you to go."

Amy began to cough again, this time more strenuously. George almost went in to try and help her, but thought better of it and held back. He needed to pull himself together first. He wasn't ready to face his family just yet.

"It's time for your medicine." Liz hurried off toward the kitchen.

"You sound lousy," Jimmy said to his sister.

"I've felt better, but I'm okay. This just isn't one of my better days." Amy made an effort to control the coughing. "Jimmy, Mom's right. You ought to try harder in school."

"I thought you would understand how I feel." Jimmy stuffed his fisted hands into his jeans pockets, much in the way that George did.

"I do understand, honest! But it means so much to Dad."

"I can't help that. He can't live his life over again through me. I know how I feel; he doesn't! Hey, let's not argue, not until you're feeling better anyhow. I'm going out back. I want to work on my tree house for a while." Jimmy grabbed his jacket and exited through the rear of the house. Amy continued to read and cough simultaneously.

George couldn't postpone any longer letting his family know he was home. He entered the living room, listening to Amy's labored breathing with concern. Liz was right; she sounded worse. George approached his daughter, bent down and kissed her on the forehead.

"How's my sweet girl today? How are you feeling?"

Amy gave him a thumbs-up and a cheerful smile. "Fine, Daddy. I hardly coughed at all in school."

"But I heard you coughing now."

"Oh, it's only since I came home." She looked down at her book. "Did you know that dolphins are mammals, not fish, and that they have a highly developed brain capacity?"

George smiled and patted her cheek. "They aren't the only smart ones."

Liz returned with a medicine bottle and spoon. "Is that a science book you're reading?"

"Biology. I took it out of the library. It's really interesting."

George turned to Liz. "I wish we could get her brother to sit down and read a book that way."

Liz turned away from him. "Jimmy has other interests."

"Yeah, like playing ball."

"There's nothing wrong with that."

"Probably thinks he's going to be a major leaguer. I did at his age." George smiled at the bitter-sweet memory.

"There's nothing wrong with that either," Liz countered.

"It's unrealistic."

"Somebody makes it. It's good to have dreams," Liz said. "Lose your dreams, and you could lose everything that matters." Her spine stiffened.

Why was she being argumentative? It was the last thing he needed or wanted to hear today. "Some dreams are just plain foolish, give you nothing but heartache."

"Jimmy has lots of abilities. He's good at making and fixing things with his hands, just the way you are."

"That's the point, Liz. Don't you understand? I don't want him to be like me. I never had the opportunity to get a college education. No one bothered to encourage me. My only ticket out of here was to join the army. Otherwise, I would have gone down in the mines like my old man. At least, I knew enough not to do that because I saw what it did to him. But if my folks had cared half as much about me as they did about Larry, I might have been successful like him today."

Liz put her arms around him. "Honey, you are successful, if only you would realize it! Why you could write the book on auto repair."

He pushed her away. "The only part of a book I'll be writing is Chapter Eleven. I'm a nobody and I got nothing!" He smashed his fist down on the coffee table. Liz and Amy watched him in silent disbelief.

"George, what's wrong with you? You're not acting like yourself." Her voice was tight.

"I don't feel much like myself. In fact, I'd give a hell of a lot to be somebody else today."

Liz turned to Amy and handed her the spoon with the medicine bottle. "Amy, dear, take this out to the kitchen. I'll be with you in a few minutes."

Amy looked from her mother to her father then went to the kitchen.

Liz then turned back to him. "All right, George, what is it? I haven't lived with you all these years not to know when something is very wrong."

"I can't talk about it right now. I've got to sort some things out in my head."

"Sorry, I'm not buying it. You better tell me what the problem is. Maybe if we talk it out, it'll help."

"No, Liz, this is one thing you can't help me with."

She faced him with determination. "I don't like it when you shut me out."

"Look, it's been a bad day, could you get me a beer?"

"Sure, but first, let's talk."

He covered his face with his hands and shook his head.

"Please, George, what is it?" She placed her hand on his. "You're scaring me."

He turned to face her. "You really want to know? All right. The garage was closed today, and it looks like it's going to have to stay shut permanently."

Liz sat down heavily on the couch. "What? I don't understand."

"You might remember hearing something about an underground coal fire?"

"Probably, but what's that got to do with the garage?"

"Seems the fire's been burning a very long time, years and years, and all that time, it's been slowly advancing toward town, until, well, it finally arrived." George sank into his armchair, overwhelmingly weary. It was as if a crushing weight had landed on him.

"You can't mean the fire's come as far as the garage!" Her eyes opened wide.

"That's what the rep from the environmental agency told me. You know I would have had the garage paid off by the end of next year. After all this time, after years of sinking everything back into the business, I was actually going to own it free and clear." He lowered his head in defeat. "What am I going to do now?"

"You're saying we've lost the business? I can't believe it!"

"Believe it."

"What about insurance? Aren't we covered?"

"I don't think so, but I'm not sure. I'll ask Larry to find out for me."

Liz placed her arms around his neck. "Honey, at least we still have the house."

George had a terrible thought and jumped to his feet. Their eyes met.

A look of horror slowly spreads across Liz's face. "The house! No, it can't be, not the house too! George, which way is the fire moving?"

"I'm not certain." The great weight was constricting his chest. He swallowed hard.

"We only live down the road from the garage," Liz said.

"Let's not borrow trouble. There's a chance it won't come this way." If only saying those words would make it true.

Liz let out a shaky breath. "I suppose you're right. I should be comforting you, not the other way around. I'll get that beer for you."

George stopped her. "Hold it a second." He

took her into his arms. "I just want you to know no matter what happens, I love you."

She smiled. "George, no matter what happens, we'll cope."

"I know that, honey."

Amy came back into the living room with Jimmy beside her.

George noticed with alarm that Amy was coughing worse than before. She was struggling to breathe. Her labored efforts terrified him.

Jimmy looked pale. "Mom, Dad, Amy came out back and she started to wheeze. She can't seem to catch her breath."

"I'll call Doc Holmes," George said.

Liz stopped him. "He doesn't have office hours today."

"Then I'll take her to the emergency room of the hospital."

"I'm coming with you," Liz said. "Jimmy, stay close to the phone. We'll call you as soon as we know anything."

George lifted his daughter in his arms and carried her out to the car. Everything else would have to wait. His daughter's well being came first. Nothing mattered more to him.

CHAPTER FIVE

The hospital emergency room had a distinctive smell that made his stomach churn. George hated hospitals, hated the sterility, the coldness of the corridors and the scent of sickness. At the floor desk, nurses looked at each other but avoided eye contact with him. When there were no relatives around to complicate their work, they probably found it easier to go about their necessary tasks. Family members made it all too real and personal.

George waited nervously with Liz. He paced the waiting area. His head had begun to throb.

"It seems like we've been out here forever. What's taking them so long?" George ran his hand through his hair.

Liz was pale. "She's never had an asthma attack as severe as this before. I'm really frightened."

George's instinct was to comfort Liz, no matter how worried he felt himself. "She'll be okay." He walked over to his wife and took her hand in his own. "That young doctor said they'd give her a shot of adrenalin. Remember when she got sick that other time? It fixed her up real good."

Liz gave a solemn nod. "Yes, I remember. It's just so scary."

She rubbed her arms as if she were feeling chilled. "Wish Doc Holmes was around. He's the best."

"It'll be okay." It had to be.

"When we were driving over here, I held Amy in my arms and I kept thinking over and over, what would I ever do if we lost her?"

George seized her by the shoulders. "Don't think that way. She's going to be all right."

Liz started trembling. "Oh, God, I hope so."

George was just as fearful as Liz, but he knew he had to appear strong. Liz needed his support.

The young doctor came out of the emergency treatment room and approached George and Liz.

Liz hurried toward him. "Doctor, how's our daughter?"

"She's going to be fine." He had a pleasant, reassuring voice.

Liz breathed a deep sigh of relief. "Thank God!" she said in little more than a hoarse whisper.

George let out the breath he'd been holding. He grasped Liz's hand. "See, I told you, honey." They fell into each other's arms.

The doctor furrowed his brow. "There is something I need to ask though. Are either or both of you heavy smokers?"

George exchanged puzzled looks with his wife.

"No, doc, neither one of us smokes. Why do you ask?"

"Because your daughter doesn't appear to be breathing in enough oxygen."

Liz gave him a questioning look. "What does that mean exactly?"

"Well, I can't be certain, but she seems to be suffering from some form of gas poisoning. Of course, I'm sure your regular physician will want to have some tests run just to get a more accurate understanding of the problem. With your permission, I'd like to keep your daughter here overnight for observation. She's pretty exhausted, and I think we ought to monitor her."

George caught Liz's troubled expression.

"Is it really necessary, doctor?"

"I believe it is, Mrs. Ferris, or else I wouldn't suggest it."

Liz turned to him. "What do you think, George?"

George didn't hesitate. "If the doc says that it's best for Amy to stay over, then I guess we should do it." George was relieved Amy was doing well. Right at the moment, that was all that mattered to him.

The young doctor spoke to Liz. "We'll take very good care of her. In fact, you can go in and see her in just a few minutes."

George looked after him as the doctor exited back through the emergency treatment room. The man had explained that something in the environment had intensified, maybe even caused Amy's asthmatic attacks. Was it the house that was making his daughter sick? He hoped that wasn't the case, and yet he feared it could be. There had been his own dizziness at the garage.

Liz worried her lower lip. "The doctor seems so young, but I guess that doesn't matter."

"Of course not. They don't let just anybody become a doctor, you know. Amy's going to be fine. Stop worrying so much. You can phone Jimmy and let him know that she's all right."

"Just as soon as I've seen her and made certain. I suppose now might not be the best time to discuss this, but it's on my mind."

George gave her a questioning look. "What?"

"Remember the other night when I mentioned I'd like to go back to work at least part-time?"

"I thought we put that idea to rest."

"You did. I didn't." Liz met his eyes with a steady gaze. "When Amy is feeling better, I want to look into the possibilities. I could brush up on my secretarial skills. There's no need for me to stay at home during the day. The children are in school most of the time. They're also mature now and responsible."

George was certain this was a result of what he'd told her earlier about having to close his gas station. "I can still pay the bills," he said, almost choking on the words.

"What's wrong with me wanting to contribute? I worked when we were first married."

"That was different."

"No, it wasn't! I want to help out with our family finances. Don't I have the right?"

George felt his anger building. His head was hurting worse. He almost let out a curse but bit back on his tongue. Men worked and supported their wives and children, while women stayed home and took care of the family. That was the traditional way of things, the way it ought to be. He thought Liz held the same opinion, but now he had to wonder. "You think I can't provide for you and the kids anymore?"

Liz put her hand up in a gesture of denial. "Did I say that?"

"My mother never worked." George raised his chin.

"Times might have been different then. Most women work these days, married or not. George, some of your ideas are outdated and chauvinistic."

"Maybe you're right, but I don't want you to start looking for a job just yet. Look, we've got some savings to fall back on. That'll carry us for a while."

"We both know you intended that money for the children's education."

"I'll replace it as soon as I can. Let's talk about this some other time. Right now, all that matters is Amy."

"All right," Liz said. "I agree. Amy's well-being is what matters most."

George placed his arm around his wife and drew her close. Liz, in turn, hugged him. Touching her comforted him. It wasn't usual for George to show affection to his wife in public this way, but he sensed they both needed it to get them through this ordeal.

CHAPTER SIX

George wasn't used to being at home during the afternoon. He walked around the living room distractedly then picked up a copy of the local newspaper, glanced at it, and tossed it down. He went to the television set, picked up the remote, hunted through the channels and eventually shut off the idiot box. He took a deep breath and let it out slowly, aware of the tension that was creating knots in his stomach. Closing the garage had nearly broken him. He couldn't seem to concentrate on mundane things.

Jimmy came bustling into the room. He dropped his schoolbooks on the coffee table.

George felt his blood pressure rising, his face flushing. "Hey, that's no way to treat your schoolbooks. Show some respect."

Jimmy rolled his eyes. "Sure, Dad, whatever."

George was in no mood to put up with Jimmy's attitude. "No wonder your mother's thinking about going back to work. It's pretty boring around here in the daytime. Even TV is dull. Either they got soap operas, game shows or moron talk shows."

Jimmy snickered. "You get a choice: greed, sex or violence." He grabbed the remote to the television set and turned it on.

George gave him a hard look. "Don't you have homework to do?"

"Yeah, but I never start it the minute I get home. My brain needs recharging. I'll do it later."

George narrowed his eyes. "How much later?"

Jimmy shut off the TV. "I've been cooped up in a classroom all day. It's nice outside. If you don't mind, I think I'll go out back and work for a while."

"You mean play, don't you?"

Jimmy's expression was one of indignation. "No, I'm working on a treehouse back there. I'm also putting together a birdhouse for Amy. But even if I were out playing, what's the big deal?"

"You never seem willing to crack a book. How are you going to amount to anything?"

"You're just taking it out on me because you lost the garage. Well, I don't deserve it. I'm almost in high school. I got a right to live my own life and make my own decisions."

He didn't want or need this confrontation with his son, but he wasn't going to back down. "You think so, do you? While you live under my roof and eat my food, I decide what's right and what's not!"

Jimmy's complexion reddened. "Screw you!"

George slapped his son across the face. Jimmy flinched and stared at him as if he were a monster. My God! What had he done? He never hit the kids. "I'm sorry. I shouldn't have done that. I apologize. It won't happen again, but you got no right to disrespect me."

Jimmy held his hand to his face, eyes wide, and his brow furrowed. He seemed shaken. "I'm sorry too, but can't you just accept me as I am? Besides, there's more than one occupation in this world."

"Yeah, sure, you want to end up like me?"

"What's so bad about that?"

George lifted his hands in the air as if to ward off the question as if it were some evil spirit. "Look at me, son. Look at these hands! They're gnarled like old trees. And what have I got to show for all those years of hard labor? I want you to be able to come home at night with clean fingernails like your Uncle Larry, not with dirty hands like mine." George held out his hands for his son to inspect.

Jimmy shook his head. "As far as I can see, your hands are clean, cleaner than Uncle Larry's will ever be."

George had to try reaching out to Jimmy again. "Son, you're not really hearing me."

"I hear you fine. I just don't see things the same as you. Look, Dad, I liked being around the garage. I always did. I see you work real hard fixing up people's cars. Fixing cars right, it's kind of like being an artist or a doctor. No one's hands are cleaner than yours. You help people and you never cheat them."

George placed his arm around his son. "You sure are a goddamn stubborn kid." He had mixed feelings, pride on the one hand for Jimmy's growing maturity, but disappointment that his son didn't value academics more.

Jimmy pulled away. "Guess I must have inherited my stubbornness from you, Dad."

"Don't get wise with me."

"I'll try not to. Can I go out back for a little while? I want to finish up that birdhouse for Amy."

"And the homework?"

"After dinner, I promise."

"Okay, I'll call you in when your mom comes back with Amy."

"Super cool. Amy's gonna love the birdhouse. You know how crazy she is about her parakeet. Imagine how she'll react when all those wild birds comes flocking here to feed."

"And I suppose you're going to be the one who cleans up all the bird crap that gets left behind?"

Jimmy looked at him out of the corner of his eye. "I didn't exactly say that."

"Well, you better."

Jimmy left through the back. George picked up the newspaper and glanced at it again. He was still edgy and out of sorts, feelings he couldn't shake. No way he was able to focus on all the bad things happening in the world when his own life was down the crapper.

A car pulled up in the driveway, and he ran to the front window to look out. Liz was finally back. He breathed a sigh of relief.

Liz came in the front door with Amy. George went to his daughter and lifted her for a hug.

"We sure missed you around here last night. Your brother complained because he had no one to argue with."

Amy turned her head to one side. "You made that up, didn't you?"

"You caught me. How are you, honey? Are you really feeling better?"

"I'm fine."

Liz worried her lower lip. "I wish we could be certain of that."

George gently put Amy down. His daughter looked pale, fragile. He would have given his own life to protect her.

"I'm okay," Amy reassured them firmly. "You and Daddy don't have to make a big fuss over me. Honest!"

"All right," Liz said, "but I want you to promise to take it very easy. Go upstairs and lie down for a little while. You've just been released from the hospital, after all. I'll bring up some juice and cookies after you've rested a bit."

"I'm really not tired."

Liz leveled her gaze on Amy. "Do as I say!"

Amy pursed her lips. "Yes, Mother." She left them and went upstairs.

Liz glanced around. "Where's Jimmy?"

"Out in the backyard. I'll call him for you."

Liz put her hand on his forearm. "No, not yet. I want to talk to you alone first."

He watched as she dropped her purse and keys wearily on an end table then sat down on the couch. There were shadows under her eyes.

"Did Doc Holmes look at Amy today?"

"He certainly did."

George didn't like Liz's grim expression. "Well, what did he have to say?"

"He seems to agree with that young doctor. They both think Amy's been exposed to things in the atmosphere that are having the effect of intensifying her attacks. Doc Holmes is very concerned. George, it has to be in the air around here."

The pains in his head were returning, sharp and insistent. "What are you talking about? There're no factories, no toxic dump sites."

"But there is a fire smoldering under us."

George ran his fingers through his hair. "And what am I supposed to do about that?"

"I don't know, except we've got to do something. We can't continue to live this way now that we know." Liz lifted her head, placed her hand to her ear and started to listen with concentration.

"Did you hear that?"

George was puzzled. "Hear what?"

Liz was on her feet now. "Listen, George! It's Jimmy. Something's wrong!"

"I'll go check." But before he could leave the living room, Amy came running down the stairs crying and coughing slightly.

"I'm scared!"

Liz took her daughter into her arms. "Calm down, honey."

"It's Jimmy, I heard him scream! When I went to the window, I saw, I saw –"

Liz held Amy away, staring into her eyes. "What?"

"Our backyard, it's not there anymore, and Jimmy, he disappeared. Something terrible happened to him!" She sobbed hysterically while Liz tried to comfort her.

"Your dad's going back there. Everything's going to be fine. Daddy wouldn't let anything bad happen to your brother."

Liz and Amy hurried to the kitchen window overlooking the backyard as he started racing down the backstairs at breakneck speed.

"Dear God, please let my boy be all right!" he whispered in a barely audible voice.

There was a large, gaping hole where the backyard used to be. He called down into the darkness. "Jimmy, can you hear me?"

Jimmy called back, though the words seemed garbled.

Liz came up to where he was standing. "My God, this is a nightmare!"

He could hear Jimmy crying out for help.

"I'm coming, son!"

Liz started to weep. "We've got to get him out of there."

"Don't you think I already figured that out? There's a strong rope in the garage. I'll bring it out. I'm going to climb down and see if I can get to him right now."

Liz grabbed his shirtsleeve. "It's too dangerous. You'll both be sucked down. I'll call the emergency number."

"No time for that. I don't think he's as far down as you think. Still, I've got to act fast."

George hurried to the garage and located the rope he thought he would need. He had to set his fears aside and deal with the situation in a calm, rational manner. Thank God for his army training. He found his strongest flashlight. He wasted no time getting back and handed the flashlight to Liz. "Position the beam down the hole so we can see into the darkness. Understand?"

Liz gave a quick nod. With that, George began climbing down. His heart was pounding and his hands were shaking. He started to cough, hardly able to breathe in the foul air. He prayed he wouldn't be too late. He smelled sulfur and could see gas rising from the depths.

"Jimmy! You hear me?"

"Dad, I can't hold on much longer." Jimmy's voice was choked. "There's a shelf here but it's not very big or very stable."

"I'm coming for you." George tied one end of the rope around his waist, knotting it securely. He kept climbing down and reaching for his son, but Jimmy was still too far away. Their hands couldn't touch. A sharp-edged rock cut into his palm as he tried to get a grip. George momentarily lost his balance and footing. He started to slip but managed to right himself at the last moment. His heart thumped like a racehorse approaching the finish line. He was panting heavily, sweating freely yet concentrating on the task at hand. All that mattered now was getting hold of Jimmy.

"Listen to me, son. I want you to reach out. You understand? Reach up to me, extend yourself."

"Can't. I'll fall!"

"No, you won't! I promise I'll get you. I'm going to get as close as I can and then toss you the end of a rope. Tie it tightly around your middle and hold on to it with one hand. You understand?"

George moved as far down as he could manage, positioning his body solidly so that he wouldn't slip again. He extended his arm as far as it would reach, then tossed the free end of the rope to Jimmy, who reached out to grasp it. After what seemed like an eternity, Jimmy called to him that the rope was securely around him.

George strained every fiber of his being to pull his son's quivering body upward until finally their two hands met and George was able to pull his son up the rest of the way.

He made the mistake of looking down only once after that, and shuddered. The hole beneath them appeared black and fathomless. They climbed to the top together, George hauling his son to firmer ground. Then they staggered further away from the sinkhole together, finally collapsing onto the ground to catch their breath. Both he and Jimmy were covered with grime. Both were exhausted. Neither could speak.

Liz aided Jimmy to struggle up the back steps and into the kitchen. George followed, still barely able to catch his breath. Once in the kitchen, Liz began wiping the dirt from Jimmy's face with a towel. "What exactly happened?"

"I don't know. I mean, one second I was hammering away, the next, the earth just sort of gave way and collapsed under me." He began to cough.

"It's a sinkhole," George explained to Liz.

"It was like some giant monster swallowed me up. I fell into this big, black hole. It was fuming and smelled like rotten eggs. I thought I was being buried alive. Kind of like watching a horror movie, only this one was real and I was living through it. Dad, if you hadn't pulled me out of there, I'd be dead!"

"Don't exaggerate. You would have climbed out on your own," George said.

Jimmy shook his head. "I thought for sure I was going to die."

Amy began to sob and threw her arms around her brother.

"He's fine, honey. Your brother's just shaken up," George said.

Liz turned an accusing look at George. "Well, I don't blame him, do you? There's something very wrong happening here. It's not safe anymore for the children. They can't stay in this house. That's definite. My sister will take them if I ask her."

"Mom, I'm not going to Philadelphia!" Jimmy said.

"You are if I say so! Your dad and I will decide what's best."

"Hell, there's no need to disrupt their schooling and send them so far away. I'll call Larry. He and Suzanne have that big house and only them living in it. I don't think they'd mind having the kids stay over for a few days until we can decide what to do."

"I know Larry won't mind, but what about Suzanne?" The way she held his gaze was intense.

"It'll be all right."

"And then what?"

"Don't ask questions you know I can't answer." Christ, she was sounding like the grand inquisitor. "Look, it's going to be okay. We'll work something out."

Jimmy stuck out his lower lip. "I don't want to stay with Uncle Larry."

"Why not?"

"Aunt Suzanne is such a snob. Her nose is stuck up so high she probably has more nosebleeds than a mountain climber."

Amy giggled. "Jimmy's right. Every time we're there, she always warns Jimmy and me not to touch anything in her fancy house."

Jimmy's color was returning. "Yeah, Dad, she's like a prison warden. And I can't stand her furniture. Everything's covered in plastic. You sit on a chair and you slide right off."

"Sometimes it seems like Aunt Suzanne is made out of plastic herself," Amy confided.

George had heard enough. "Your mother believes it isn't safe for you in our house anymore. Like it or not, I'm going to have to call and make arrangements for you both to stay there for a few days."

"Please, Daddy, don't do it!" Amy began coughing again.

"End of discussion. It won't be for very long, honey, I promise. Just until we figure out what to do. Besides, the doc told your mom you can't breathe well here. Uncle Larry lives up in the hills. The air is clean there."

George went over to the telephone hanging on the kitchen wall. He dialed and waited for the phone to ring. It was picked up on the second ring.

"Lawrence Ferris, attorney-at-law. How can I help you?"

"Hello, Miss Lynch? This is George Ferris. Could you please put me through to my brother."

There was a pause at the other end of the line.

"Miss Lynch? Did you hear me?"

"Yes, Mr. Ferris. Your brother is with a client." Larry's secretary sounded reluctant, but he was in no mood to put up with any crap.

"Look, this is important."

"Mr. Ferris, as I explained, Larry is busy at the moment. If you give me a message, I'll be certain he gets it." The crisp, business-like tone of Larry's assistant was too much.

"Look, this is urgent. I need to speak with him now." George smacked the wall with his fist. "I'm sure his client can wait an extra minute." George drummed his fingertips against the wall as he waited. He was relieved when his brother's deep baritone finally came on the line.

"Hello, Lar. Your secretary tells me you're very busy, so I'll get right to the point. Could you and Suzanne let the kids stay at your house for a little while? We're having some problems. Liz feels it's dangerous for them to remain here. It's got to do with the fire." He quickly explained what had happened during the past few days. As he'd expected, his brother was sympathetic.

"I'm glad you phoned. I was going to call you later. There's going to be an emergency meeting of the town council tonight to discuss what the fire is doing to the town. They'll be talking remedies. They say a rep from a coal company is going to make some recommendations. Maybe offer some solutions. I'll be there. Make sure you come too."

"I wouldn't miss it. Thanks." George felt a glimmer of hope.

When he got off the phone, George saw that the others had been listening and watching. "We're all set."

Amy stamped her foot. "I don't want to stay at Uncle Larry's."

Jimmy stood up beside her. "Neither do I!"

George looked to Liz. She gave him an imperceptible nod, indicating she would handle the situation. That was Liz: He could always count on her to deal with the kids.

"You're both being unreasonable," Liz said, looking from one child to the other.

Amy shook her head. "Mom, Aunt Suzanne doesn't like us very much. She's going to be angry."

Liz gently stroked her daughter's hair. "Things aren't always as they seem, dear."

Jimmy spoke up. "Aunt Suzanne is cold and uppity. That's the way it seems and that's the way it is."

"People who don't have children of their own are often uncomfortable around them."

Amy frowned "She could have her own children, couldn't she? I think she's just too selfish to want any."

"We don't know that. Anyway, you won't be staying there for very long – just until your dad and I figure out what to do." Liz placed her arms around both her children and hugged each one to her in turn. "No matter what, we're a family. Always remember that. We love each other, and that's what really counts. I'll call you a lot, and you promise to do the same for me."

"All right, Mom. Can I take Pretty Girl with me?"

"Better leave her here for now. I don't think Aunt Suzanne would appreciate having a parakeet around. I'll take good care of her. Honor bright." Liz kissed her daughter and then her son on the cheek.

George came toward them. "Everything's taken care of. Larry's going to phone Suzanne right away. You kids go upstairs and get packed. I'm taking you over there soon."

Jimmy and Amy exchanged looks. "Can't we wait until tomorrow?"

Liz glared at them. "You heard your dad!"

Jimmy groaned, but both children walked up the stairs, even if it was at a reluctant, slow pace.

George turned to Liz. "Finally there's some potential good news. Larry told me the town council has called a special meeting for tonight to discuss the situation the fire is causing in town. We aren't the only ones affected, you know."

Liz shrugged dejectedly. "Talk is cheap, and that's all the council ever does, unless there's some money in it for them."

"God, Liz, when did you become so cynical?"

"Why shouldn't I be? They could have put that fire out years ago. They just didn't care."

"According to Larry, the town couldn't afford to do it."

"Then where will they get the money now that it costs so much more?"

George puts his arm around her. "Honey, don't be so down. It's going to be all right. We've got to believe that."

"I wish I could. Our children are both in danger here, and I would hate to think that we have to lose both the garage and the house." Tears welled up in her eyes, then overflowed down her cheeks. George touched one tear with his fingertip, brushing it gently away.

"Maybe we won't have to lose them. Larry said something about a representative from a coal company coming to the meeting. Larry seems to think something is in the works. Maybe they're going to offer to assist us."

Liz tossed him a dubious glance. "In exchange for what? Coal companies have never been confused for Santa Claus. Why would they help us?"

"I don't know, but I'm going to find out. I'll be at the town council meeting tonight. Larry's coming too. Do you want to be there with us?"

"No, but I'll wait up for you. Then you can fill me in and we'll discuss it."

"Are you sure? You might want to ask questions I wouldn't think of. You're smarter than me."

Liz shook her head. "Larry will ask the right questions. It's been a difficult day. I'm feeling tired and sick to my stomach. I'd rather rest. Still, I can't help worrying that the house may no longer be safe."

"Take it easy. The house is on pretty solid ground. I have the feeling things are going to start looking up for us." His conversation with Larry had, for the moment, alleviated some of the despair he'd been feeling.

"I hope to God you're right." Liz's expression was grim.

"I want to hold you in my arms and reassure you, but I need to take a shower first. I'm a mess." George glanced down at his soot-covered clothes. His jeans were ripped over his right knee, which was cut and bleeding.

"Toss Jimmy in the shower as well."

George smiled. "Will do."

As he washed away the grime and got ready to

drive the children to his brother's house, George was preoccupied, wondering if the coal company would act as their saving angel or turn out to be just another devil. He'd kept a positive, optimistic attitude for the sake of his wife and children when he wasn't feeling much in the way of hopeful himself. For their sakes, he couldn't give in to fear and doubt. They were all suffering. He needed to be strong for them. They needed his support and he was determined not to let them down.

CHAPTER SEVEN

George glanced around the room from the doorway. Chairs had been set up, as was a table, a speaker's platform and a podium. George didn't usually attend the town council meetings. He mostly viewed the yammering of politicians as pointless posturing. The chambers struck him as official looking, Larry's proper domain, not his. Several people were standing around gabbing to each other. George entered, caught sight of Larry, and motioned to his brother.

Larry waved and nodded. Then he excused himself from the two men with whom he'd been talking, and approached George. "I'm glad you're here early too."

George glanced at his watch. "Early? It's nearly eight o'clock. Aren't they supposed to get started in a few minutes?"

Larry shrugged. "Theoretically, but these things never begin on time. We need a chance to talk anyway." Larry gestured to some empty chairs and they sat down together.

"I can't thank you enough for letting the kids stay over."

"Hey, I am their uncle." Larry smiled good-naturedly.

George hesitated but he needed to ask. "And Suzanne, she didn't kick up a fuss after Liz and I left?"

Larry hesitated. "Suzanne will be fine. Besides, right now we have other matters to discuss."

"What about the insurance?" George didn't like his brother's expression. Larry was frowning.

"I looked into it. Your policy doesn't cover this disaster."

"I figured they wouldn't want to shell out, but I'm up to date on my payments. Aren't we covered for fire damage?"

Larry wet his lips in an uneasy manner. "The thing is, they're saying you weren't insured for a pre-existing condition. I don't suppose you happened to purchase state insurance from the Mine Subsidence Authority?"

"What are you talking about? I never heard of that."

"Your insurance agent probably should have mentioned it."

George's spirits sank. No help from insurance. That sucked. But maybe there could be other possibilities.

"You found out more about the coal company?"

Larry raised his right hand. "Hold on. I don't know all the facts and details yet. However, I was assured by the mayor that the company's representative is going to offer us some kind of deal."

George stood up. "That's great! Maybe they'll come through for us. I told Liz I had a feeling that things were going to somehow work out okay." He so hoped it was true.

Larry stood up beside him. "We haven't heard them out yet."

"You lawyers don't trust anybody." He took a moment to look around. "A lot of my neighbors are planning to be here tonight. I called a few people before I came."

"I expect things to get pretty heated. There's no doubt that everyone affected by the fire is going to exert pressure on the council."

"I intend to do my full share."

Larry pointed at a man George didn't recognize. "Look over there. You see that distinguished-looking fellow in dark-framed glasses? That's Francis Logan, the representative of the coal company."

"You were talking together before I came into the chamber."

"We've had some business dealings. Francis is a lawyer too. I better warn you. If he were any shrewder, they'd probably have to write another commandment just for him. I'll bring him over. Just remember to be careful what you say to him."

"Hey, I'm not a little kid. I don't leave drool on my bib or pee in a diaper."

"No, but you can be blunt and forceful. With people like Logan, you need some finesse."

"That's your department. Look, I know I can be crude sometimes, and maybe I'm a little rough around the edges, but I talk straight, and I value that in other people too."

"Noted." Larry gave a quick nod.

He watched Larry approach Francis Logan, and then the two lawyers chatted out of earshot. Afterward, Larry brought the other man over to George. Logan was youthful although conservatively dressed in a business suit. George was conscious that his own appearance didn't measure up.

"Francis Logan, I'd like you to meet my brother, George Ferris. I was wondering if you could explain your company's proposal."

Logan gave him a smarmy smile. "I plan to do exactly that, but during the council meeting."

Larry smiled right back. "Can't you give us the gist of it now?"

Logan concentrated on removing a thread from his suit jacket. "My presentation is rather involved."

"But you could give us some idea, couldn't you? It would mean a lot to George. He's suffering because of the fire."

George chimed in, "I've already lost my business, and I could lose my home."

Logan didn't appear unsympathetic. His eyes met those of George. "I can fully comprehend your dilemma."

"Can you? Don't think so unless you've been there."

Logan looked from George to Larry then gave a quick nod. "Very well, I suppose there's no harm in telling you. Our company is prepared to put out the underground fire that's plaguing your community. I will set a detailed proposal before your town council this evening."

That sounded too good to be true. George had accused Liz of being cynical, and maybe her attitude had rubbed off on him, but he was feeling skeptical. "The rep from the environmental protection agency told us it would cost a hundred million bucks to put out the fire. Why would your company be willing to do that for us?"

Logan took out a clean, white handkerchief, removed his eyeglasses and slowly wiped them, obviously not eager to answer questions. "You're right, our motives are not altogether altruistic. There's still iron ore, a deep rich deposit under this town."

"I see. You put out the fire and in return, the town shows its gratitude by letting you mine the ore."

Logan carefully folded his handkerchief and placed it back in his pocket. "Something of the sort." The response seemed evasive to George.

"There is more to it. Am I right?" Larry said.

Logan fidgeted. "I think it's time for me to take my seat now. It would appear they're about ready to begin."

Larry wasn't ready to let the other man go just yet. He placed his hand on Logan's arm. "If you don't mind, I want a bit more information about the iron ore."

Logan, a head shorter than Larry, cleared his throat, then pulled at his shirt collar as if it felt too tight. He didn't make eye contact with Larry and edged away from him. "Very little to tell really. According to our geological surveys, the iron deposits are under the town."

"Then how do you intend to mine the ore? Surely you don't plan to dig up the entire town?"

The two lawyers locked gazes.

"That is exactly what we intend."

George fisted his hands. "That's crazy! It doesn't make any sense!"

Logan gave a long-suffering sigh. "Hear me out, gentlemen. You are probably unaware that in order to put out the coal fire, we have to excavate more than half the town."

George exchanged an astonished glance with his brother.

"Are you certain of that?" Larry asked.

"With so much money involved, I'm very sure. Our survey was thorough. The fire is spreading from west to east. The entire western section of this town is beyond salvaging."

George sat down heavily on an empty chair as the painful realization sank in. "So I've lost it all? The garage, the house, my hopes and dreams for the future, all going up in smoke."

"There is a bright side to this," Logan said. "Our company is prepared to make a generous offer to every resident for his property."

George looked up. "Full value?"

Logan's tone was cautious. "Let's just say it will be a reasonable offer, under the circumstances."

"Well, I guess that's better than nothing. At least there would be some money to start over somewhere else. The town's been expanding north into the hills. Maybe we could afford to move there."

"You may be a bit premature. You see, the company insists that everyone in town agree to sell their property. Otherwise, they will buy none of it."

Larry stared at Logan in open-mouthed amazement. "Everyone must sell? I don't follow the logic. Why is that necessary?"

Logan blinked much as an infant would. This was a deceptive tactic, George realized. "The company insists on securing complete rights to the area."

"Why not just the rights to the area directly affected by the fire?" Larry persisted. "Those of us who live in the newer homes in the hills aren't involved in this problem. Surely your company doesn't intend to include us in its proposal?"

"But we do. My instructions from the company are quite explicit."

Larry stamped a foot in frustration. "That is incredible!"

"I am sorry, but the company demands all or nothing. You will excuse me now, won't you? You'll have an opportunity to discuss this later."

Logan quickly walked away from them then took a seat in the front row, near the dais.

George turned to Larry. "What do you think, Lar? Will people go along with it?"

"Probably only those personally affected by the fire will want to sell." Larry glanced away as he bit down on his lower lip.

The strength seeped out of George. He was tired, so tired, and weary. "Politicians and big shots do a lot of talking, but little guys like me, we get screwed no matter what."

Larry didn't respond. For once his brother was out of glib, easy answers. What was going to happen? George shuddered

CHAPTER EIGHT

George found Liz asleep on the sofa when he returned home. She thrashed around in her sleep, moving awkwardly on the couch, then let out a low moan. Liz cried out, "No!"

George tossed his keys on the coffee table. Liz jumped up with a start.

"Didn't mean to wake you, hon. Sorry."

Liz rubbed the sleep from her eyes. "Don't be sorry. I was having a horrible nightmare."

"What about?"

Liz sat back, her spine straight and stiff. "I dreamed I lost my balance and found myself sliding into a deep, dark hole, you know, like the black pit that's in our backyard now. Anyway, I couldn't seem to stop falling. It kept getting darker and darker. And I kept falling deeper and deeper. Then I thought I found the heart of the fire. I wanted to put it out. Around me were flames everywhere. I realized the fire was consuming me.

Then I saw you and the kids, but I couldn't reach you. I wanted to cry out a warning before it was too late, but the fire seemed to have us all. And as we began to burn, I suddenly looked around and I realized exactly where we were." Liz stared into his face, shivering, and her expression one of horror. "George, we were in Hell! Burning in fire and brimstone, condemned for eternity, and there was no way out. The fires of Hell were consuming our souls along with our flesh and blood." She began to sob uncontrollably. George took her into his arms and tried his best to comfort her. He kissed her hair and then her eyes. It broke his heart to see her like this.

"Take it easy, Liz. It was just a dumb dream. It doesn't mean a thing."

"It was so real!"

"Nightmares always are. Now that you've told me about it, it'll be forgotten. You'll feel better once you get a good night's sleep." He glanced around. "I'll close that window for you. That sulfur smell from the hole in the yard would give anybody bad dreams."

Liz was trembling when he came back to join her after closing the window. "I saw steam coming out of it before, and you are right about the smell.

With the windows closed, maybe it won't seem so bad. I'm glad Jimmy and Amy aren't here tonight, but I do miss them badly. The house is so quiet without them, like a tomb."

George took her hand and held it tightly in his own larger one. "Hey, this situation is only temporary."

"How did the council meeting go this evening?"

George dreaded telling her about it. Liz was suffering enough. "All right, I guess."

Liz studied him. "You don't sound as enthused as you did before you left."

George fisted his hands and stuck them into his pants pockets. "Well, the coal company did make us an offer. They want to buy out everyone's property."

Liz brightened "They do?"

"How would you feel about moving?"

"Wither thou goest."

George hugged her. "I'm really lucky to have you for my wife. Maybe I should tell you how much I love you more often than I do, but I've never been much with words. I know you could have married a lot better than a dumb guy like me."

Liz frowned at him. "I wish you would stop putting yourself down. You're a wonderful man." She tried to hug him back, but he held her off.

"I know that you and Larry were once close."

Liz turned away from him. "That was a very long time ago."

"But we never really talked about it."

"How did you know? Did Larry tell you?"

"No, it was Ma. She mentioned it once, thinking I knew."

Liz turned back to look him in the eye. "It was over before you ever came back from the army, before I even knew you."

"I always kind of wondered."

"Then why didn't you ask?" Her eyes widened.

Now it was his turn to look away. "Guess I was afraid." The thought that Liz might have preferred his brother was too painful to consider.

"You had nothing to fear."

"That wasn't what I thought. Was it because of Suzanne? The breakup, I mean?"

He looked at her again, and Liz squirmed.

She turned away from him. "It seems foolish to discuss it after all these years. What difference does it make?"

"I don't know, but it seems to me that when people have been married as long as we have, there shouldn't be any secrets between them. There shouldn't be any subject we can't discuss."

Liz folded her hands together. "Some things are like Pandora's box, best left closed."

"So it still hurts? You still got feelings for Larry, don't you?"

Liz stood up. George had upset her. "I don't want to talk about it."

Her reaction was disturbing. It troubled him that she didn't trust him enough to give a straightforward answer. "It's been between us all these years."

"I don't believe it! You're actually jealous of a relationship I had with another man nearly twenty years ago?" Now she sounded defensive as well as irate.

"The fire started around that time too, but it's affecting our lives this very second."

Liz pointed an index finger at him. "That's not the same thing, and you know it."

"The hell it isn't!" George took Liz by the shoulders, forcing her to face him. Suddenly he felt impotent, emasculated.

"All right, since you're so eager to know about Larry and me, I'll tell you, although there isn't much to tell. Larry and I dated for a while when he was home from law school one summer. I was working as a legal secretary for old Mr. Ryan in those days. Larry came in to apply for a clerkship. That was how we got acquainted. We dated that summer, but it was never serious. Maybe it might have been, but he went back to school in the fall. At first, he wrote frequently, then not so much. Finally, not at all. I saw your mother one day in the grocery store, and asked her how he was. She told me he was getting engaged to a girl who lived close to the university."

"Suzanne?"

Liz gave a quick nod. Her lips narrowed.

"The only thing Suzanne ever had over you was her family's money. Larry was always impressed by wealth. He hated being poor. I remember when we were kids, he used to say he was going to dig down in the mines and strike gold."

"Well, Suzanne's father is certainly rich and influential, but I think there was a lot more to the attraction. Suzanne is beautiful and sophisticated."

"Says who?"

"Come on! It was never much of a contest. I'm just a drab sparrow in comparison."

"Now who's the put-down artist?"

She smiled momentarily, but it was a small gesture, as if she discounted what he had to say. "As long as we are being open with each other, there is something I would like to know."

"Ask away."

"Did you start dating me in the beginning because you knew about Larry and me?"

The hurt was a knife twisting into his heart. "I thought you knew me better. When you came into the garage, I recognized you from high school. I liked you even back then."

"You were a senior, an athlete, and I was only a skinny freshman. I didn't think you ever even looked at me."

"Oh, I looked all right, but I was too shy to ask a girl out in those days, even one as pretty and nice as you. The army helped me build self-confidence."

"So if I hadn't smashed my fender, we might never have gotten acquainted?"

George shrugged. "I guess not. It wasn't until I told Ma we were getting engaged that I found out about you and Larry."

"And it didn't make any difference to you?"

George took her hand. "It made me realize that there was at least one thing I was smarter about than him. You were and are the most desirable woman I've ever known."

"I'll take that as a wonderful compliment, but George, you've got to stop feeling as though you're in competition with your brother. You're every bit as good as he is, and you don't need to depend on him for anything."

Her tone cut into him. "Don't lecture me, like I'm one of the kids." George started toward the front door. He couldn't talk to her about this anymore. He wouldn't! He was convinced he loved her more than she loved him. Maybe he'd always known it. Maybe she'd only settled for him because she couldn't have his brother.

"Where are you going?"

"Out of here, I need some fresh air to clear my head."

"Wait. Don't go!" Liz sounded alarmed.

"I can't stay. I'm in a rotten mood, and I don't want to take it out on you. If I stay, I'm afraid we'll have a quarrel. I don't want that and neither do you. I'm going for a walk."

"But it's so late!"

Bitter bile filled him. "You forget. I've got no place to go in the morning. It doesn't matter when I get to bed."

Liz still seemed intent on stopping him. She followed him to the front door and grabbed his arm. "I'm sorry! I'm not feeling very well. I had a headache all day. I might have said something wrong."

George paused, his hand on the doorknob. "You said what you meant. You don't have to be sorry. Maybe I'm not the smartest guy in the world, but I understand. You married me as a substitute for Larry, didn't you? No, don't answer that! I don't want you lying to me."

She tried to go toward him, to reach him with her touch, but he put up his hand, turned quickly and exited. As he slammed the front door, he could hear Liz crying, and he felt like a rotten scumbag. Nice going! How had he managed to take his misery out on the one person he loved more than anything or anyone in this world? But he needed to be alone for a while to clear the cobwebs from his head. He hoped a walk would help him sort things out—one way or another.

CHAPTER NINE

Liz was again sleeping on the sofa when George quietly entered the living room. He studied her for a few moments and decided not to disturb her. "Okay, I'll let you rest," he muttered. "Christ, it seems close in here!" George went to the kitchen to fix himself a sandwich. He was still too much on edge to consider going to sleep. Even the long walk he'd taken hadn't helped.

George glanced at the birdcage on the kitchen shelf and did a double take. Pretty Girl was lying on her back, feet straight up in the air. He picked up the cage and shook it. The parakeet didn't stir. Christ, it looked dead! His hands weren't steady. He carried the birdcage into the living room.

"Liz! Do you know what happened to Pretty Girl?" He got no response from her. "Honey, wake up." Liz still didn't move. He was becoming agitated. "Please speak to me. I know you're angry, but don't ignore me this way. Amy's parakeet is dead! My God, what am I going to tell her? Liz, come on, get up! Speak to me!" She still didn't stir. "Hey, if you're getting even with me, you can stop it right now!" He shook her gently. "Honey, wake up." Still no response. He dropped the birdcage. "Liz, let's go up to bed. Look, I'm real sorry I lost my temper before. Liz, are you all right? Damn it! Open your eyes! You're scaring me!" George tried to shake her again, this time sharply, but she remained unresponsive. "God, what's happening?" His heart was pounding. He was terrified. He could hardly breathe, but he had to think, to act.

He rushed to the telephone and quickly dialed. "Hello, this is an emergency; I need an ambulance right away!"

■■■■■■

George paced, occasionally looking up at the emergency room sign. He was aware that he appeared distraught but didn't care. Doc Holmes eventually joined him. The appearance of the elderly, unpretentious man who had been their family doctor since he could remember was reassuring.

"Doc, how is she?"

Doctor Holmes placed his arm around George. "I'm not certain yet, but you did a good thing rushing her out of the house and administering CPR."

"She didn't seem to be breathing, and it was so close in there. I thought if we waited outside for the ambulance, it might be better for her."

"You were absolutely right. It may have saved her life."

George slumped, feeling as if he were being further crushed by a heavy weight. "But you don't know?"

"Not yet. We're doing everything we can for her. There are very good people on staff at this hospital."

"She's got to be all right!"

Doc's eyes were filled with compassion. "I'll be back again soon."

"I appreciate you coming out in the middle of the night to help us."

Doc Holmes offered a tired smile. "Just part of the job. In the meantime, can I have a nurse get you anything? Maybe some coffee?"

George shook his head then continued to pace after Doc Holmes left him. He wasn't certain how much time had passed before Larry hurried toward him.

"Are you okay?"

"It's not me I'm worried about, it's Liz!"

"How is she?"

George shook his head. "We don't know yet. I think she might die!"

Larry placed his arms around George, who was grateful, feeling as if he were ready to collapse.

"Hold yourself together. Liz is a strong girl."

"That's what everyone thinks because Liz wants it that way, but she isn't really all that strong. She looked so delicate tonight." George regretted the way he'd spoken to her before he left for his walk earlier. He placed his hands over his eyes. "God, I'm sorry." He looked over at Larry. "And I never should have bothered you at this late hour of the night. You didn't tell the kids, did you?"

"No, there didn't seem to be any sense in waking them up. Tomorrow is soon enough to find out about this. Besides, by then, maybe there will be some good news."

"Sorry about waking Suzanne."

Larry offered a careless shrug. "She understood."

"Did she?" He searched his brother's face.

"Sure, besides, if nothing else, at least I can be here to lend you moral support. Remember when we were in high school, and I used to go to all your football games? I was certain that if I wasn't there, your team would lose. So I always came and cheered."

"Tonight, cheer for Liz." George almost choked on the words.

"Look, it's going to be a long one. I'll go to the cafeteria and see if I can't get some coffee for us. Just try to keep calm. Liz will make it."

George pressed his callused hands together. "If she doesn't, I won't want to go on living."

"You can't think that way. You've got two terrific kids who need you. You've got to think about them."

"The last time I saw her, we sort of had an argument. I was angry with her. I'd give anything to tell her how sorry I am. All I want to do is hold her in my arms and tell her that I love her. What if I never get the chance?"

Larry bowed his head and didn't say anything for a while. "I'll get the coffee," he said eventually, subdued.

After Larry left him, George walked back and forth, running his hands through his hair. He wasn't certain how long he did so, but eventually Doc Holmes returned and again put his arm around George. He stared into the doctor's eyes with trepidation.

"Doc, what is it? How is she? She hasn't—"

"No, no, she's better. She's going to make it."

"That's— That's great! I don't think I've ever been so damn frightened in my entire life."

"She's going to be fine."

"When will I be able to bring her home?"

"You can't. As a matter of fact, neither one of you can stay in that house anymore."

George lifted his brow in confusion. "I'm not following you, Doc."

"It's the fire. One of the products of combustion is carbon monoxide. It's being released into the upper atmosphere as the fire burns. It nearly killed Liz tonight. She was deprived of oxygen and nearly smothered to death. If you hadn't found her when you did, she would have died. At the very least, in just a few more minutes, irreparable brain damage would have occurred."

George stared at him in horror and amazement. "I can't believe it."

"Well, it's true, just the same. Every family on top of that fire has to get out quickly."

"That means losing our home."

"Better than losing your life. Anyway, you've got no other choice. Carbon monoxide is odorless, tasteless, invisible and deadly, a silent killer."

"Christ, my wife and children could have died." George put his hands over his face again.

"But they didn't. You're a lucky man."

"Funny, I don't feel lucky. When will they put the damn fire out? Or are they waiting for someone to die?"

"Truthfully? That's how it usually works. The government will finally step in and do something if enough people are asphyxiated, and that's only because it creates bad publicity. There has to be a public protest, a human outcry. Then they begin to listen. Public officials only act if enough pressure is exerted on them."

"I feel like going after some of those guys with a gun. They got no feelings, no compassion. All they understand is what touches them personally. All they understand is fear."

Doc viewed him with a stern expression. "Take it easy! Don't let your temper get the best of you. That's crazy talk and it doesn't solve anything. Just makes everything worse."

Except it was better to feel anger than despair. Anger made him want to act, while despair left him feeling impotent and pathetic. But he sensed there was no point trying to explain this to Doc. Hell, he didn't really understand them himself.

"When can I see Liz?"

"We had to work on her a long time. She needs to rest for a while. Why don't you get some sleep and come back late in the morning."

"You forget, Doc, I got no place to go. Besides, I want to stay near her. I didn't know what I had until I almost lost it."

Doc Holmes left him just as Larry returned. He handed George a paper cup of coffee.
"I saw Doc leave. Did he have any news?"

"She's going to be all right."

"George, that's terrific! Liz is really okay?" Larry was beaming.

"According to Doc, she'll be fine. I can see her later. She's sleeping now."

"What happened to her?"

"It was because of the fire. She nearly died of carbon monoxide poisoning."

"Jesus!"

"It was my fault. I never should have let her stay in the house, not after what happened to the kids."

"You didn't know. You, Liz and the kids can stay with us until we work something out."

"I don't want your charity or anyone else's."

"I wasn't offering any. Aren't I allowed to care what happens to my own family?"

"If you really want to help me, there's only one way."

"What's that?" Larry's eyes grew round behind his gold-rimmed glasses.

"See to it that something comes of the coal company's offer."

Larry let out a low whistle. "You don't ask for much, do you?"

"What about your neighbors, Lar? Can you get them to go along with it? You got a gift for convincing people. Everyone says you know how to work a jury."

A brief, uncomfortable silence followed, in which Larry's gaze was downcast.

"I know it won't be easy, but you can persuade them, Lar. I know you can."

"It's not that simple."

"I got it all figured out. When you talk to them, you tell them what's right. They'd have your example to follow. That'll carry a lot of weight."

Larry cleared his throat. "George, you know our house really belongs to Suzanne. I talked to her about this earlier when I first got home. She isn't willing to sell her home, not for what the coal company is offering."

George stared at his brother open-mouthed. "Let me get this straight. My own brother won't sell?"

"*Can't*, not won't!"

"You're telling me that your own wife won't listen to you?"

"Suzanne has a mind of her own."

A deep sense of betrayal took hold of him. George crushed the paper cup in his hand; he barely felt the hot liquid spill over his palm. "Get out of here!"

"Calm down. You don't mean that."

"The hell I don't!"

"I'm trying to help you. I care about you and your family."

"You're a liar! You only care about yourself." How could Larry of all people justify what he and Suzanne were doing? Traitorous bastard!

Larry raised his hands as if to ward off a raging bull. "Maybe I'd better leave. There's no point trying to hold a rational discussion with you when you're like this." He threw his own coffee into a garbage receptacle.

George called out after him. "Yeah, go, run back to your rich bitch." Then he muttered to himself. "God, give me strength!"

CHAPTER TEN

George heard the knocking at the front door and then the voices. He decided to let them wait. He was in a peculiar mood, confused, angry and bitter, all at the same time. He could hear Larry clearly now, but George continued to lurk in the shadows near the dining room, not ready as yet to speak to his brother again. The two days that had passed since he last spoke to Larry hadn't really helped him come to clear-cut decisions. He had something in mind now but wasn't certain if it was the best way to handle things. Still, he was the kind of person who felt best when he was acting rather than passively accepting a bad situation.

"George, are you there?" Larry knocked again. "George!" He heard Larry try the front door and then enter the hallway.

"We shouldn't just walk in." Suzanne had come with Larry.

"The door's not locked. Besides, George is expecting us."

"He calls and we have to run over here. What a miserable way to spend Saturday morning."

"Frankly, it sounded urgent."

"Fine, why did I have to come along?"

"Because he specifically asked if I would bring you."

"I wish he would stop bothering you. Ever since we've known each other, he's made demands on you. Now he's really getting outrageous."

"Honey, George is my brother."

"Like a lot of people, he confuses kindness for weakness."

"George isn't like that. There isn't anything he wouldn't do for me if I asked him."

"Please, he considers you a soft touch. He plays on you like a violin. The more you do for him, the more he demands. The man's insatiable."

"Be quiet...please! Look, I'm sorry to drag you into this, but I'm really worried about him. You didn't see how erratically he behaved at the hospital. I think he's near the breaking point. We had this argument. He never talked that way to me before. I want to try and patch things up with him. Maybe it'll help."

"All right, but where is he anyway?"

"I saw his car out front. He's around here somewhere. George?" Larry walked out to the kitchen then quickly returned. "He's not in the kitchen." George watched as his brother went toward the stairs. "George, are you up there?" Larry stood and listened. "He might be out back. Stay here. I'll go through the mud room and check."

"Is it safe to even be in this house, after what happened to Liz?" Suzanne raised a tissue to her nose.

"George has the windows open. It's okay, at least for a little while."

After Larry left, George observed Suzanne standing in the middle of the room, hugging her body and glancing around with apparent disdain. George stepped forward into the living room. Suzanne must have heard his footsteps. She turned and stared at him.

"There you are! Larry went to look for you outside. Didn't you hear him call to you?"

"I wanted a chance to talk with you privately first."

"I can't imagine why. You and I have nothing to discuss."

"I disagree. There's the matter of the coal company's offer."

She gave him a hard look. "Why did you really want me here today?"

"Why do you think?"

Suzanne's hands shook as she removed a pack of cigarettes from her purse.

"I wouldn't light that in here if I were you. There's no telling what might happen."

She dropped the cigarettes back into her purse.

"Your children have been asking for you."

George felt immediate concern. "Are they okay?"

"Fine. Larry took them to the hospital to see your wife. Where were you?"

"I saw Liz after she came out of it. Since then, I've been doing some thinking, trying to sort things out."

"That's no excuse. Your children need to see you."

Larry returned to the living room. "There you are! George, you okay? You look awful."

"I've been sleeping in my car the last couple of nights. Guess I haven't given much thought to appearances."

"The kids were upset because you haven't been by the house."

"Just tell them I love them."

"I think you ought to be the one to do that."

"I've been going over it all in my mind, Lar, but I can't figure a good way to handle things. You were always the smart one. What would you do in my place?"

"Come back to our house. This is no place to talk about anything."

"No, this is the right place. You're smart, Lar, help me figure out what I should do."

Larry shook his head. "Maybe I had a better education, but I'm certainly not more intelligent than you."

"You're not answering my question."

"Because I don't have a solution."

Suzanne took a step toward him. "Well, I do. We would be happy to loan you some money, as much as you need to start over again somewhere else."

"You figure that would buy off Larry's obligation to me?" His tone of voice was harsh.

Suzanne let out a deep sigh of annoyance. "Exactly what obligation is that?"

"Maybe you don't know, but he does."

Suzanne gave George an exasperated look. "This is absurd! Larry, can't you see how he's trying to take advantage of you?"

Hatred flooded George. "Suzanne, all you know about is money. You reek of green stuff! Your old man must have cut your heart out and stuffed you with hundred dollar bills."

Suzanne pointed a well-polished fingernail at him. "I'll ignore that because I know how jealous you are. Must you always run to Larry with your problems?"

George took a confrontational stance. He pointed an accusing finger at her as if it were a gun. "You're a spoiled, selfish woman, and it's a good thing you were never able to have any children. You would have made a terrible mother."

Suzanne began to tremble. "That's a lie. I chose not to have children. I didn't want any little brats like yours! You go straight to hell!"

George smiled bitterly. "You forget, I'm already here." He indicated his surroundings.

Larry placed his arm around Suzanne. "George, you're being hurtful and intentionally cruel. I've never known you to talk to anyone this way."

George ran his hands through his hair. "I'm not the same person anymore." He turned and confronted Suzanne again. "It's because of you that the deal with the coal company is going to fall through. The others would sell if you did, but, no, you're too selfish!"

Suzanne faced him, her cheeks flushed. "You're pathetic!"

Larry raised his hands as if trying to conciliate. "Don't you see? This is just what the coal company had in mind when they made their offer. It's a form of extortion. They're trying to use the people affected by the fire to coerce the rest of us. For God's sake, George, don't play their rotten game!"

George felt like throwing up. "Is there any other?"

"Larry, please, let's just leave. I don't see that we have anything more to talk about."

"Maybe you're right. Maybe talk won't help. Action is truer. You know, when I was up in the attic, I ran across some of my old army stuff. Things were simple for me then. They handed us some weapons. They told us who the enemy was, and we tried to shoot them. These days, I'm not so certain who or what the enemy is."

George reached into his pocket and withdrew a revolver. He pointed it at Suzanne. She gasped, and Larry moved himself protectively in front of her.

"What are you doing with that?" Larry asked.

"If words can't persuade Suzanne, maybe this will. I'm ready to use it." He wasn't certain this was the right way to deal with Suzanne, but he knew she wouldn't respond to weakness. The weapon in his hand gave him a sense of power, a way to deal with the enemy like in wartime.

"You ungrateful cretin! You Neanderthal!" Suzanne was livid with fear as well as anger.

Larry squeezed her hand. "Insults won't solve anything."

"How can you be so calm?" Suzanne's eyes filled with tears.

"Trust me, I don't feel calm, but ranting and raving aren't in anyone's best interests."

Larry then turned toward him. "What's happened to you? Have you become mad?"

"My whole world's turned inside out. Maybe I have gone nuts."

"I want you to put that thing away. Threatening people is foolish and pointless. Even if you could get Suzanne to change her mind about selling the house, most of our neighbors wouldn't agree. You can't threaten all of them."

George's hand was shaking. "You're mighty smooth with words, Larry, but words don't solve anything."

"Neither does violence. Put the weapon away, and let Suzanne go. You have me here. You and I will work this out."

George stared down at the gun barrel. "I don't think we can."

"Of course, we can figure this out together. Just like when we were kids."

"When Amy was about four years old and Liz had just got done feeding her, Jimmy walked in from the yard and announced he was starving. Amy turned to him and said: 'How can you be hungry when I'm full?' I don't think Suzanne or even you, Larry, can have any idea of how I feel right now. I'm running on empty while your bellies are full."

"Maybe I don't understand, George, but I do love you. Let Suzanne go so we can talk. Okay?" George nodded. Larry turned to his wife. "Just wait for me in the car. Don't call anyone!"

George watched Suzanne hurry out. He still

clutched the gun. He might have been able to kill Suzanne but never Larry.

"George, we would like to make you a loan, one that you can pay back when things settle down."

George was despondent, crushed. Was this what Larry thought: that he was hitting up his younger brother for charity? Did Larry think this was some kind of play for pity? How had it come to this? How low had he sunk in his kid brother's esteem? His eyes glazed over.

"Suzanne's right, you know, I have been jealous of you for years. You got an education and I didn't. I always knew how the folks felt about you. They gave you everything. They wanted so much for you. Pa was always boasting about your academic achievements. He was so damn proud! Just once I wish he talked that way about me."

"Be honest, George. You could have gone to college too. In those days, you never wanted to study. You conveniently forget. I earned my own spending money working as a janitor at the college. And as for tuition, I won a scholarship. The folks didn't really have all that much to give. I didn't take advantage of them. I never made demands. I worked very hard for everything I got. As for the way they felt about you, the last words Pa uttered on his deathbed were: 'I hope George is all right'."

"I never knew that." He was touched by Larry's revelation. Tears welled up in his eyes.

"How could you know? You were still in the army. By the time you got back, it was all over. Mom and Dad worried about you constantly when you were overseas. Pop asked me to tell you not to become a miner no matter what. He didn't want you to end up like him. It weighed heavily on his mind those last days. You still think he didn't love you?" Larry shook his head sadly. "Like you, Pa wasn't much for words, but he cared. As for me, well, I guess I always knew how you felt. You managed to make me feel pretty damn guilty over the years. Maybe that was my own fault. If you're going to shoot anyone, it might as well be me."

"No, I was wrong. I wasn't thinking too straight." What was he doing? George stared down at the weapon in his hand as if he were holding a cobra.

"Then give me the revolver. There's no need for it. Let's just forget this." Larry held out his hand for the gun but George moved backward, shaking his head.

George spoke in a strained voice. "There's nothing left, Lar. Don't you see? I'm losing my business, my home, everything I've worked so hard for all these years." It was all gone.

Larry moved cautiously toward him. "You've still got your family. You'll never know how much I envy you that."

"They would be a lot better off without me." George turned the weapon on himself, pointing the gun at his temple. There wasn't much point to his life anymore.

"Don't do anything foolish. Liz needs you. So do the kids! They depend on you."

"When a man loses his self-respect, he's got nothing. I'm ashamed of myself. I never should have threatened Suzanne or you. Just felt so desperate."

"Please, I'm begging you. Put that thing down." Larry made an imploring gesture with his hands.

"If I were dead, maybe Liz could collect some insurance money."

"They don't pay off for suicide. Forget it! I'll find a way to help you, I promise."

George shook his head. "You're not your brother's keeper. Time to face facts, high time. I'm nothing but a failure."

"No, you're not."

"This isn't your problem, not anymore."

"You disappoint me. I never thought self-pity was your style. I thought you'd fight it out no matter what the odds. That's what I've always admired about you."

"Guess I get credit for teaching you something you didn't know. I'm afraid, Lar. Fear's caught me by the throat like a pit bull and won't let go. I can't let Liz or the kids see me like this. A man's got to have some dignity, some pride, otherwise, he's better off dead." George pulled back the hammer to cock the revolver. He felt his hand shaking.

"You're not a failure, George, a fool, maybe if you pull that trigger, but not a failure. Only a fool would consider throwing away all that you've got."

"Don't you see? I don't know if I can start over."

"You can; you will. I know one thing for certain: If you deny yourself to your wife and children, you'll be depriving them of the most important thing of all. I always believed that of the two of us, you were the strong one. Remember how you were never afraid to fight anyone, even the bully a head taller than you? Remember that kid? What was his name? You know, the one who used to extort lunch money from me and all the littler kids?"

"Butch Davis."

Larry gradually came closer to George "That was him. Except for you, everybody was scared to death of him. But you took him on and you beat him up. Nobody ever gave him a cent after that. I felt awfully proud to be your brother. I'm still proud. You're not a coward. You can't run away; you've got to fight back! You never gave up in the past; you can't now. We'll fight this, we'll fight it together." Larry embraced George. He allowed his brother to take away the gun. "You're going to survive. It's going to be all right."

George wanted to believe Larry. Could he find a way to survive with some level of self-respect? To start over again? He would have to find the way, somehow.

CHAPTER ELEVEN

George and Liz entered the living room of the house that had been their home for so many years. George had his hand on her elbow for support. Two days had passed since that fateful, emotion-filled meeting with Larry and Suzanne in this very room. Afterward, George had cleaned himself up, gone to see Liz in the hospital, and then much as he disliked going there, visited his children at Larry and Suzanne's home. He was trying his best to pull himself together for the sake of his family. Larry was right; they needed him. He should never have considered taking a coward's way out. He must never give up.

"You look much better, George." Liz smiled at him, running her hand over his shaved cheek.

His hair was combed and he was wearing a fresh shirt. It wouldn't do to have his wife and children see him in a distraught, disheveled state. He needed to be strong. Liz too seemed rested, but there was sadness in her face. There were several gray hairs where none had existed before. He had placed the suitcases they'd packed next to the couch.

Liz glanced around. "I guess that does it for now for you and me. There are so many things we're leaving behind."

George placed a reassuring hand on her shoulder. "We'll be back for them once we're settled."

Liz let out a deep sigh. "I better go back upstairs and see how the kids are doing with their packing."

"Relax! This is your first day out of the hospital. You're supposed to take it easy. Packing your own stuff was more than enough."

Liz frowned. "I don't know if I can relax. Everything seems so strange, so surreal to me."

George took her hand and guided her to the couch. "Sit down for a minute. Besides, I want to talk with you before the kids come down." He seated himself next to her on the sofa. "I promised myself that if you were all right, I'd tell you how sorry I was. I know what happened to you was my fault."

Liz shook her head so vehemently, her hair moving like a wheat field in the wind. "That's not true." Tears formed in her eyes that she tried to brush away.

"Honey, please don't cry! I love you. I always have." He held her hand and put his arm around her. "Seems I don't say it enough, but I do love you and the kids very much. Forgive me. I'm grateful you're alive and well, and that you've come back to me."

Liz pressed her forehead against his. "I loved you from the first day we met. Maybe I don't say it enough either. Maybe I don't show it. I regret that. I found out something. I found out how vulnerable I am, how fragile we all are." She moved back and looked at him. Her deep, dark eyes held his, growing more intense as she continued to speak. "To just simply drift off to sleep and never wake up again. It can all happen so quickly. It's only when you get a second chance that you begin to realize how precious every moment actually is."

"Christ, it must have been awful for you."

"No, I hardly knew what was happening to me. Dying isn't frightening after all; it's facing life that's difficult." She turned those dark, sad eyes on him again. "Oh, George, what are we going to do? We can't live in this house ever again."

"I know, honey." He patted her head in a soothing gesture.

"The thought of leaving here frightens me."

"Me too," he admitted. "I'm not someone who handles change well."

"In the hospital, I was thinking about Job in the Bible. Remember how he never knew why all those terrible things were happening to him and his family? He didn't know that God was testing him. I want to believe things happen for a reason. What do you think?"

"I don't know, Liz. I don't have your kind of faith, and I'm not what you'd call a deep thinker. How many people have died senselessly in this world? It doesn't add up for me."

"But I think there has to be a reason," she persisted, her expression earnest.

George shook his head. "I don't know if that's true."

"I've been giving it some thought. I believe that I was spared so I could do something worthwhile with my life."

"Like what? You do so much for the kids and me already."

Liz shrugged. "I don't know exactly. Maybe

help other people understand about the fire. If people find out about us, maybe they'll start to care, and then maybe something will be done. There're so many environmental disasters. People have to start caring. They have to be made to see that things have to change so that our children and their children can have decent lives."

George stood up. "I don't think people care about anyone but themselves."

"Then we have to make them understand that it could happen to them just as easily. Maybe not a fire, but with all the toxic dumps and pollution in this world, everyone's in danger. Water, land, air, everything's being poisoned. If they remain apathetic, we're all doomed! Don't you see? We have to make what's happened to us matter somehow."

Liz was becoming agitated, and he didn't like it. She was still weak. He wanted to calm her. "All right, honey, I guess we can try."

Amy and Jimmy came downstairs carrying their suitcases. George went to take Amy's luggage. Liz rose and approached them.

Jimmy gave them a toothy grin. "We're all packed."

George gave him an approving nod. "Good, then I guess we're ready to go."

Liz looked around, tearful again. "It's hard leaving this house. It's been our home for so long, I can hardly bear it."

George placed his arms around her. Amy and Jimmy came up to their parents.

"We're just glad to have you back, Mom." Jimmy hugged his mother.

Amy smiled, looking from one to the other. "It's okay. We're only leaving our house behind. We're taking home with us."

Liz embraced both children as George continued to hold her. As they clung to each other, George realized his brother was right: Family was what mattered most. They would manage in a new place because they were together. As Amy had said, they were taking home with them.

About the Author

J.P. Seewald is a multiple award-winning author, and has taught creative, expository and technical writing at Rutgers University as well as high school English. She also worked as both an academic librarian and an educational media specialist. Seventeen of her books of fiction have been published to critical praise, including books for adults, teens and children. Her short stories, poems, essays, reviews and articles have appeared in hundreds of diverse publications and numerous anthologies such as: *The Writer, The Los Angeles Times, Reader's Digest, Pedestal, Sherlock Holmes Mystery Magazine, Over My Dead Body!, Gumshoe Review, The Mystery Megapack, Library Journal, Publishers Weekly,* and *The Christian Science Monitor.* She's also an amateur landscape artist and enjoys listening to blue grass music. She loves hearing from readers. Her writer's blog can be found at: jacquelineseewald.blogspot.com.

About the Publisher

Annorlunda Books is a small press that publishes books to inform, entertain, and make you think. We publish short books (novella length or shorter) and collections of short writing, fiction and non-fiction.

Find more information about us and our books online: annorlundaenterprises.com/books or on Twitter: @AnnorlundaInc.

To stay up to date on all of our releases, subscribe to our mailing list at:

annorlundaenterprises.com/mailing-list

Other Titles from Annorlunda Books

Short eBooks

Caresaway, by DJ Cockburn, is a near future "inside your head' thriller about a scientist who discovers a cure for depression, but finds that it comes at a terrible cost.

Unspotted, by Justin Fox, is the story of the Cape Mountain Leopard and the author's own journey to try to see one.

The Lilies of Dawn, by Vanessa Fogg, is a lyrical fantasy novelette about love, duty, family, and one young woman's coming of age.

Okay, So Look, by Micah Edwards, is a humorous, yet accurate and thought-provoking, retelling of the Book of Genesis.

Navigating the Path to Industry, by M.R. Nelson, is a hiring manager's advice on how to run a successful non-academic job search.

Don't Call It Bollywood, by Margaret E. Redlich, is an introduction to the world of Hindi film.

Collections

Hemmed In is a Taster Flight collection of classic stories about women's lives.

Missed Chances is a Taster Flight collection of classic stories about love, all with a hint of "the one that got away."

Love and Other Happy Endings is another Taster Flight of classic stories, all of which end on a high note.

Small and Spooky is a Taster Flight of classic ghost stories, all of which feature a child.

Academaze, by Sydney Phlox, is a collection of essays and cartoons about life in academia.